About the Author

Baylee Morgan grew up in Pleasant Grove, UT, surrounded by family and friends. She is currently in the process of getting her undergraduate degree. She has a love of music and animals that continues to grow, along with her passion for literature.

8th Grade Butterflies

Baylee Morgan

8th Grade Butterflies

Olympia Publishers
London

www.olympiapublishers.com
OLYMPIA PAPERBACK EDITION

A CIP catalogue record for this title is
available from the British Library.

ISBN: 978-1-80439-001-6

This is a work of fiction.
Names, characters, places and incidents originate from the writer's
imagination. Any resemblance to actual persons, living or dead, is
purely coincidental.

First Published in 2023

Olympia Publishers
Tallis House
2 Tallis Street
London
EC4Y 0AB

Printed in Great Britain

Dedication

I dedicate this book to all the 8th grade graduates, and the friends who turn into family throughout the years.

Acknowledgements

Thank you to my family and the Azuas, I couldn't have done this without you.

Chapter 1

Jordan Myers was the last person I wanted to see when I walked into my local grocery store. The minute we laid eyes on each other, thoughts came crashing back into my mind. My last real memory of him flooded my mind as we made our initial contact. We were at our eighth grade dance, something I had been looking forward to all year long, when he told every boy I had on my pre-assigned dance card that I forgot to put deodorant on. This normally wouldn't be a huge deal at this age, but the week before the dance we had been given 'the talk'. The one they tell everyone around that age, about hygiene for our bodies, among other things.

The night of the dance, all but one of them only danced with one hand on me, the other plugging their noses at my "stench". It was humiliating. If it wasn't for the pre-assigned dance partners, I don't think anyone would have danced with me thanks to him. The one and only boy who didn't plug their nose became my best friend, Russel Laketon. I was so grateful to have a small, but needed break from the humiliation that night, and I repaid Russel through friendship. Since then Russel and I have hung out every single day since that night. That is, until we grew up and got jobs and hobbies. Since then, we have seen each other at least twice a week for dinner and a movie. He was there for me through everything, including Jordan Myers's relentless teasing the week following the dance.

Then came eighth grade graduation. I remember that day so

well, like it was only yesterday. I don't know if everyone has an eighth grade graduation, but it was one of the happiest days of my life (sad, I know). We all cried and hugged, and partied right after receiving our useless cheaply made diplomas that stated 'Graduate of Wallace Charter School' as if we would all hang them on our fridge for years to come. And they were right: my mom still had that wrinkled and stained paper hanging on the fridge with a magnetic bottle opener that is still completely unused till this day. Unfortunately, this seemed to be the only accomplishment my parents were proud of.

All of Wallace town was very tight knit; many of the people who moved here settled down and never left. However, plenty of people my age seem to have moved to neighboring cities. I still run into people I went to second grade with every now and then, and they always remember my face, as if I still look like that eight-year-old they went to class with. That is something I can always count on: if we had met in the past, they would still remember me when we saw each other in the future. I couldn't say if this was just my round features that made me look the same, or if it was what made Wallace so unique.

The start of eighth grade was ten years ago, next month. I still remember how nervous I was on my first day, it was the last year before High School to be completely fair. Since I went to a charter school, many of the people from the previous year's class filled up this year's roster. It was unusual for it to change dramatically which only made new students stick out like a sore thumb. Only a few new faces were in the crowd, two new boys, and two new girls. The new girls and I instantly became new friends, playing constantly with each other at lunch and after school. Their names were Jamie and Lyla. They both left the district where we resided in the following year, so we quickly lost touch. Jamie's parents found a job closer to the rest of her family, and Lyla left to cut down on gas costs, according to her parents, but who would come to wallace if they didn't live in wallace?I don't really know if that is accurate, but it is what went through the grapevine.

The boys that had joined our class, Jordan Myers and Russel Laketon, were not the type of people I normally hung out with. They were loud, obnoxious and sometimes downright mean, and was quiet, reserved and a people pleaser. I still am. So I stayed clear of them until that dance the following May, where I had no choice but to interact with them. Which despite my resentment for Jordan, his plan to embarrass me in front of everyone, ended up giving me my best friend for the years to come.

Russel and I moved from school to school together until college, where we went to separate colleges only one town away from each other. He got into the state's 'smart school' for his almost perfect 4.0 GPA and extracurriculars. Meanwhile, I was getting my education degree in the local community college, despite my financial dreams. I learned right after ninth grade that I wanted desperately to be a teacher. It took me a while to finally go after what I wanted, but at age twenty-three I was basically starting over and getting my degree in elementary education. After beginning nursing school, I decided I only liked little people.

We both still lived in the town of Wallace in the same apartment complex (the only one in the town), only a few floors away from each other. We did this intentionally, so that even if life got busy, we wouldn't have an excuse not to see each other. He lived with his long-term girlfriend who we both met in our senior year of high school. You could tell he was instantly starstruck the day he met her, I can only imagine the movie montage scene going through his head. He went on for days about this girl he had met in his biology class, and when he finally got the nerve to ask her out it was game over. Laura was one of the kindest, funniest, most genuine people I had ever met, not to mention she puts up with my constant complaining, nights on the couch in her apartment and my emotions which can tend to be extreme.

Russel only had one girlfriend before, Amy, but she tried to tell Russel not to hang out with me anymore, on the account that I was a girl (that girl had no clue what she had just asked). She was gone the next day, and that is how I knew our friendship was going to last forever. Russ and I's friendship was unbreakable; nothing had ever come between us, and after all this time I don't think anything would.

I could always count on Russ and Laura; they were always there right when I needed them. Except right now, it seems.

My cans flew to the floor, and when I bent down in my high-rise skinny jeans, and oversized T-shirt to pick them up, a hand appeared.

"No, let me. I wasn't watching where I was going, I'm sorry." It was a low and deep voice, that which you would typically hear on the radio, or in a sports stadium not that I really listened to radio, or watched sports. I looked up, only to find a tall, (maybe 6'2", maybe even taller) figure standing up, cans in hand.

"Thank you," I said, standing back up, meeting his deep brown eyes, that looked somehow light like honey, and deep like an oak tree at the same time. I realized within a few seconds, who was standing in front of me. Holy crap. It's Jordan Myers.

I hadn't seen him since that night at the dance, and it had been a blessing in disguise. Who knows how I would have handled high school if he had stuck around. He had embarrassed me so much that I hadn't gone to a dance until my senior year which Russ dragged me to with Laura, reluctantly. There had been a few other attempts by Russ and Laura, but none were successful.

Jordan had gotten attractive, or maybe he wasn't that attractive and there just wasn't that much to find in this town. Either way, I couldn't stop looking at him, and I hated it

"So, are you from here?" Jordan said, not breaking the elongated eye contact, which had gone on far too long.

"Am I from here?" I said, shifting my eyes to the bent cans he was handing me, breaking the awkwardness of our stare.

"...Yeah, I mean, that's what I asked," he said, realizing that some of the cans were dented from impact, and giving them a scowl as if that would fix anything. My mind shuffled and I paused before answering. He didn't remember me. We had met before, in fact we had been long sworn enemies before. Am I that forgettable? No, that can't be it; everyone remembers me, even if we had met ten years ago or even before. I'm not exactly someone you forget. I tend to make very impressionable first impressions.

I sigh heavily, "Born and raised, never left, don't plan to." It was the unfortunate truth, I was used to Wallace, no matter how depressing it may be at times. He looked at me with a concerned raised brow, as if examining my face. Maybe he had recognized me, but he didn't say anything. Then I looked down, where his eyes were slowly but carefully going. I had spilled a giant can of tomato sauce all over my Donny Osmond T-shirt my mom had given me for my twentieth birthday.

"Crap, this is my favorite shirt!" I angrily whispered to myself.

I see Jordan's face light up with amusement. "Donny Osmond… Really?" I could feel his eyes back on my face, but wasn't going to check to see if they were there. I ignore his thoughts about the singer. I had lived with the ridicule my entire life, one more opinion won't change anything. Especially if it came from him.

"Yeah, he makes amazing music, but the 80s are really his prime time." I started grabbing the brown paper towels hanging from the side of the shelf in the aisle we were in, hoping I could at least clean up the floor before it stained.

He grabs a few from my hand and starts helping without asking.

"You don't need to… I mean, it's really not a big deal, I've got it," I say, my dark black hair hanging in front of my face.

"This was my fault, the least I could do is help you clean it. I owe you a new shirt too. Where does one get a Donny Osmond shirt?"

I snickered without replying, and watched his mouth slowly rise to a smile. That smile could be deadly, and I don't know if it's because it makes me physically ill to see him, or if it's because it is one of the best smiles I have every seen.

We finished cleaning up, and headed to a nearby trash can to discard the now red stained wet paper towels. I make sure to cup my hand under them in case they drip at all.

Walking toward the checkout line, I realized he hadn't gotten anything yet, or at least that I could see, and there was nothing for him to scan.

"Are you getting anything?" I hesitantly asked. I didn't want to seem nosey. I don't want to seem like I care if Jordan Myers gets anything in the grocery store.

"Oh shoot! The strawberries. Thanks for the reminder!" I

watch him walk, maybe more of a jog, into the produce aisle. Hoping that was the end of the conversation, I spotted him in the corner of my eye. He jogs back toward me, a little worn out.

"Here, let me know where to buy a replacement and I'll get it sent to you." He hands me a business card, his face plastered on it, winking as he places it in my hand. What an unsightly thing. I examine the card and its rough edges. It seemed like the card had been in his pocket for a long time, and he had finally gotten the chance he wanted and gave it to someone. Although, he probably should have given it to someone who would have used it.

"No need, but thanks," I say as I stuff the blue and white card into my back pocket. He doesn't reply, just heads back to the produce section to grab his strawberries.

I finish checking out, and head out to my '07 Hyundai Elantra. The stench of tomatoes still overwhelms me. I open the worn-down driver side back door and toss the cans that had not broken in the back seat. When I shut the door it jams, and I open and close it about three more times before it finally seals. This is something that happens frequently. This car had over two hundred thousand miles on it and didn't run as well anymore. In my mind as long as the car turned on and got me from point A to point B, it didn't matter that it made a rumbling sound on the freeway.

I open the driver side door, slide into my seat and play the same game, once, twice, three times before the driver side door fully shuts. I think that there is something wrong with the door seal, but that was for a mechanic to worry about. I sit there silently without turning on my car.

"What just happened?" I say to myself, looking at my hands, unknowingly waving in the air around waist level, as if telling a story. I put my hands down, which takes more effort than you would think. 1:32 P.M. my phone screen reads. Any minute, I think to myself.

Russel called me every day on his break at work. He was a technician at a software startup a few towns over. I couldn't tell you what he actually does, I just know he doesn't have to wear nice clothes to work, and is smart when it comes to computers. It was really nice that he was tech savvy, because my works IT team took hours to fix problems.

My thoughts are interrupted when my phone rings and plays the default ringtone assigned to my cracked iPhone. I bob my head along to the music, but quickly realize I need to answer my phone.

"Finally," I sigh to myself and slide the answer bar at the bottom of the phone, getting little slivers of glass under the skin of my thumb. "Russel. You will not believe what just happened. I was in the grocery store and I was getting sauce for tonight's pizza festivities when..." I get cut off by his voice.

"That's great, that's great, but I have to tell you something!"

I allowed the interruption, because surely his news was more important than running into Jordan Myers at the grocery store. Anything and everything was more important than running into him.

I turn my car on and place my phone on the passenger seat on speaker while Russel is telling me about something that happened at work, and head on my way home. My car creaks at every stop light with every attempt at breaking. I zone back into the conversation.

"...then they offered me a promotion!" I should probably have listened to the rest of the conversation; I have no clue what he is talking about. I don't know what was distracting me so much.

"Wow! Congrats!" I say back. I hope he can't tell my lack of awareness in my voice. No one deserves a promotion more than Russel; he worked all the time, when he wasn't at home listening to my rants. "What's your new title, Mr. Technician?"

"Manager of IT developments, I get to run the technician team."

"You deserve it," I say, truthfully; he does. I may not know a lot about technology, but I do know that when my printer breaks and I'm doing an assignment for class I always have someone I can count on to fix it.

We continued talking about our days, but I neglected to mention my grocery store run in. I decided I wanted plenty of time to tell him about it, and we were on a time crunch. By 1:59 P.M. his break was over, and I hadn't even remembered most of the conversation.

"Love you, Annabelle!" I heard him call through the phone's speaker. I roll my eyes with distain at the comment. No one but my immediate family calls me by my full name, and they know I hate it.

"It's Anna, and love you too!" A click happens, indicating the call is over, I realize I had been sitting in my assigned parking spot in front of my building for at least fifteen minutes, listening as Russel went on about every detail of the promotion, and how he was offered it. If I am completely honest, I don't remember any minute of the drive here, which probably wasn't good. I get out of my car after shutting it off and go to the back seat to retrieve my dented cans. I had picked up tomato sauce, olives, and canned pineapple to make scratch pizza tonight. Laura and Russ were in charge of everything else. I wasn't much of a cook, so they did the right thing when not entrusting me with anything but sauce and toppings.

I walk into the lobby with my grocery bags in hand and hit the cracked up arrow that sat in gold plates next to the elevator. I lived on the second floor of an 80s-built apartment complex that looked like it wouldn't hold much longer. I I fumble to get my keys with one hand out of the brown satchel that covered my stained T-shirt. Unlock the door and enter a mess. I wasn't the cleanest person, but I had my moments. Though they are far and few in between. I set my plastic bag filled with my purchased items on the counter; it thuds even though I try and set it down carefully. I hung my satchel on the coat rack that held pretty much everything but actual coats and jackets. I started making my way towards the back of the apartment and opened my bedroom door; it was in immaculate shape. I don't know why I could keep my room so clean, but every other part of my apartment was so dirty.

I shuffled my shirt off and threw it in the full hamper. I was grateful I hadn't done my laundry yet, because I didn't want my room to smell like tomato sauce for days. I threw on one of my many Hard Rock Cafe shirts that I own. My family collected them wherever we went, and I kept every single one. I look at the mirror and rub my rosy pale skin that doesn't have a trace of makeup on it, leaving it flushed and uneven. I only wore makeup when I went to events or special occasions, so I was definitely not wearing it to a grocery store. I throw my long locks into a messy bun and start cleaning around my apartment. I put the pillows back on the couch, and cleared the dishes from the coffee table, and set them in the sink.

I went back to my room and dragged my hamper to the washing machine and threw in a load. I heard it whir in the background as I listened to the radio station 'Donny Osmond's greatest hits' and did the dishes. Once the dishwasher was loaded,

I looked at the time; it was around three P.M. I had about two hours before I would make my way to the fourth floor to Russ's apartment. Making my way to the now clean living room, I prop myself onto my tan upholstered couch I got from Goodwill. I turned on the T.V. and started watching Spongebob Squarepants. I may be twenty-three, but it is still my comfort show.

The washer stops whirring, so I transfer my wet clothes into the dryer and throw a dryer sheet in.

"Aw man!" I realized this was my last dryer sheet. I start the dryer and head over to my fridge, where I have the shopping list I try to ignore until it's long enough to warrant making my way to the store. The list consisted of only a few things, toothpaste, deodorant, command strips, and a few other essentials. I add a sloppily written "dryer sheets" to the bottom of the list with my pen. I look at it, and realize I should go to Walmart tomorrow to grab the items on my list despite the fact that I hate any sort of human interaction. The local grocery store only had food items, and not some of the other essentials I would need. I sigh and aggressively sit on the couch with the worst posture ever.

An hour passes and I realize I'm crying at an episode of a cartoon sponge who has lost his snail. I wipe my tears under my thick rimmed glasses and head to my room. I take my glasses off, set them on the nightstand near my old full-size bed and wipe my hazel eyes, now red from crying. I knew that it was almost time to head upstairs, so I threw on a sweatshirt and took my messy bun out and re-do it. I make a stop in the bathroom for my contacts, it was the only thing that kept me from falling asleep on there couch. I always wore a sweatshirt to Russ's house; he kept it at sixty-six at all times, claiming it was the most 'comfortable temperature'. Me and Laura always tried to sneak the temperature up a few degrees, but it's like Russ had a sense for every degree, and within fifteen minutes he would walk up to the thermos and change it back down. Me and Laura would always look at each other with disappointment, knowing we would never be able to wear a shirt in this home without a jacket.

Five o'clock couldn't have come soon enough. I had been anticipating telling Russ about what happened at the grocery store. I get giddy as I walked to the door, grab my groceries and phone and head to the elevator. I press the button and impatiently wait for the doors to open. Not many people lived in this complex; it's what made it so homey, you almost never had to wait for elevators, and knew all of your neighbors' names. My hoodie strings swung as I rocked side to side. My sweatshirt stated 'hottest chick around' with a baby chicken behind the words. The doors open and I quickly make my way inside, not paying any attention to my surroundings. I reach my pointer finger on my free hand over to the large white number four when I notice it's already been pushed.

I know everyone on the fourth floor, so I assume this is someone I also know.

"How are you doing, Anna?" I hear a voice say to me. Russel's next-door neighbor looks at me with his old eyes that have definitely been through a life to live.

"Great, Mr. Hidi, how are you doing? Wife still not feeling well?"

He looks at me and gives a silent nod. He and his wife have been in and out of retirement communities, but switched to home care about two years ago when they moved into this building. If I had to guess he was around eighty-five, and I knew his wife was a few years older than him, so I knew her time was coming. No one talked about it though; they were the sweetest couple, always letting us borrow random ingredients for our cook nights, so we had gotten to know them well.

We both get off at level four, him letting me off first, and making idle chit-chat on the way to the doors right next to each other. He lived in 405, and Russ lived in 403. He entered his apartment slowly and carefully, while I knocked on the door waiting for Laura to open the door.

"Goodnight, Mr. Hidi."

"Goodnight, my dear," Mr. Hidi replies halfway through the doorway. I knew he was in his home all the way when I heard the door creak shut.

Suddenly, Laura opens the door. "Oh, thank goodness. Russ is throwing flour everywhere." I chuckle as she grabs my free wrist and swings me inside.

She was right, there was flour everywhere. Russ had decided to make the dough from scratch. The man is dedicated what can I say? The rolling pin was on the floor, rolling towards me, when Russ turned around, his dirty blonde hair covered in the mixture.

"Hey!" he said, coming in for a hug.

"No way, Jose, not happening." I put my hand up in protest. I did not want to have to change for a second time tonight.

He looked at me with sad eyes and made a little pouting noise.

I ignore it and start handing the bag of canned goods to Laura. "Here you are, my king and queen."

She laughs as she looks in the bag. "What the heck happened to these? Did you get into a tussle with the olives?"

"They came at me first!" I started laughing with her, when I realized that I had important things that needed to be shared.

"Oh my gosh! I almost completely forgot about that. Guess who I ran into today at Jamies's?" Jamies was the grocery store I had been going to since I was a kid in one of the dark green shopping carts, flinging my legs back and forth. I remembered the smell of the fresh baked bread from the bakery, and it suddenly put me at ease, despite what I was going to say to them next.

They both looked at me, eyebrows raised waiting for me to answer.

"Jordan Myers." I say with intensity and overall disgust.

Laura asks who that is, while Russ starts cleaning up the flour that covered the kitchen head to toe. I explain with very few words, while Russ silently nods along. Usually Russ would be all over an interaction like this, but I ignore his silence to answer Laura's questions.

"Woah. He gave you his business card? Did he not recognize you?" Laura stood with her arms crossed, occasionally unfolding them to gesture with her hands.

"I don't think so," I say reluctantly, but in my mind I'm hoping he would have remembered my face. I shove the thought quickly from my brain, telling myself not to let thoughts like that happen again. Just because an attractive man and I had an interaction, it does not mean anything.

"Are you going to message him?" Russ asks quietly, breaking the awkward silence. I shake my head. Why would I? There isn't a point in messaging someone when I know that all it would do, is open old wounds.

It may sound dramatic, but that dance was really what made me who I am today. I learned to stop caring, that along with my family life made me realize I don't care what other people think, I can't.

"I don't need that right now. I'll replace my own T-shirt." My thoughts have now made this situation very depressing, but I try not to let it show on my face.

Laura scoffs as she switches places with Russ behind the counter and starts rolling it with the rinsed off rolling pin. "That is not why he gave you that card. He thought you were preeeeettty," she says shaking her hips, taunting me.

I started giggling, but I couldn't tell why. Was I laughing because the thought of Jordan Myers thinking I was pretty was impossible…? Or because I wanted Jordan Myers to think I was pretty? I ground myself in my mind for having another one of those thoughts, that I just told myself not two minutes ago not to have.

I don't even know this man anymore, and what I did know did exactly help his reputation.

The subject changes after the conversation dulls. "So, did your big promotion come with a big raise?" I ask, raising my voice slightly in pitch.

"It did in fact, I now make two dollars more an hour." A half smile still stuck to his face. He knew that wasn't what he deserved, but he seemed to be ok with that amount of money.

"Great, that means you guys can pay for our hangouts now." They both chuckled, knowing they paid for most of the food we devoured twice a week anyway.

I only worked on weekends. School consumed most of the time throughout the rest of the week. I worked for a data analysis company who combed through data from other random companies to look for errors. Since both school and work were both from home, (I signed up for online classes so I would have more flexibility in my schedule) it meant I spent most of my time without human interaction. That made me inherently more awkward than most.

I had always been very outgoing as a kid, talked to everyone, wanted to be everywhere, wanted to see everything. The minute

I became an adult and realized how awful people can be, I stopped wanting those things. Russ and Laura were the only people who could convince me to leave the house, and even when they did it was never for very long at a time. I tried to limit my interaction to bare necessities at most.

I left around nine P.M. Since it was Wednesday, Russ had work in the morning, and so did Laura. I was hoping that I could get some sleep, but after today, I didn't know if I was going to sleep for 12 hours straight or not sleep at all.

I try to enter, or more stumble into my apartment, while trying to carry the leftovers from upstairs. I sink my key into the lock and it doesn't budge. I try twisting it with more force when it snaps in my hand. Who knew I had that amount of strength in me?

"Of course," I whisper to myself. I set the cooling pizza on the floor, along with my phone and other belongings. I try and take my key out of the lock, but my hand kept slipping off, as if it wanted me to suffer. "Freaking lotion, who wears freaking lotion anymore." I look at my hands, upset that they had been recently moisturized.

I try once more to take the key out, and cut my hand on the cold metal that was more sharp than it looked. It didn't hurt, but it definitely needed a Band-Aid. I licked the small amounts of metallic blood off my hand and fished for a Band-Aid in my satchel. Always prepared. I slap the Band-Aid on and pick up my items, now covered in the filth from the hallway outside my apartment.

The pizza had gotten some debris on it from being in the corner. I picked it up and frowned. "My pizza." I said with a sad tone. I start heading towards the elevator at the end of the carpeted hallway. I toss my pizza in a trash can located to the left, and press the up arrow. I look down at my dollar store bandaid that had elmo on it. They had run out of anything with cartoon characters.

I hope with every piece of my being that my two friends located on the fourth floor hadn't gone to bed yet, though it wasn't an impossible thing. They were like an old married couple: they got up at the crack of dawn, and fell asleep before the clock struck ten.

I rock back and forth on my heels as the elevator slowly rises beneath my feet. It comes to a stop on the fourth floor promptly. Most people would be spooked by how fast this thing stops, but I've lived here long enough to be used to it by now. The doors swing open, and I make my way a few doors down the hall. The lights are off inside.

"That can't be good," I whisper to myself with very little hope left. I knocked a few times, as quietly as someone can knock without the chance of someone not hearing it. No one is coming to the door. I wait a few minutes and try again. Still nothing. I turned on my heels and headed back to the elevator. I'm sure I could call and that would wake them up, but I have an irrational fear of inconveniencing people.

Pressing the down arrow this time, the elevator doors take a while to open, meaning someone must be getting off or on from a different floor. I hope no one got on; I've had enough stress for the day, I don't need human interaction to make it that much worse. The doors open as loudly as they could. I squeeze my eyes in anticipation, and only open them when the doors are fully ajar. No one's there. I take a sigh of relief and go in and press one. There was no point in going back to my apartment when I couldn't get in it. I decide I'll go to hostel Castino's across town, and call the locksmith first in the morning.

The doors start closing and are almost completely shut when I see a hand shoved through them. My heart quickens. I'm hoping it's someone I know, otherwise they may try to interact with me. The doors creak open again, and I make eye contact with the stranger. Or what I had hoped to be a stranger.

"Mr. Myers, nice to see you," I say, trying to not give any hint that we had met years ago. I hoped he couldn't hear how fast and loud my heart was beating, because it was at a very rapid rate at the current moment.

"Jordan, call me Jordan," he says with an outreached hand. I look at his hand, then promptly back at him. The last thing I'm doing is touching Jordan Myers on purpose. He slowly retracts the hand and stuffs it in his khaki pockets.

"Where are you going on this fine July evening?"

I don't answer. I looked at him, confused. I had never seen him in this building before… In fact, I hadn't seen him anywhere in Wallace for over ten years.

Still without answering, I meet his gaze again, his deep dark gaze. I stare a little too long, when he clears his throat, obviously aware that I'm staring.

"Why are you here?" It comes off more rudely than I intend, but the question is still something I want answered. I face back toward the elevator doors waiting for a response.

"Visiting my grandmother."

I scoff at the word 'grandmother'. No one I had ever met that wasn't a filthy rich person called their grandparent 'Grandmother' or 'Grandfather', it was always shortened. The alternative seemed so impersonal.

"On the fourth floor?" I ask, keeping my gaze on the elevator doors. I want to look at him, but given my brief and new history, I know that I have trouble keeping my eyes on him for too long.

"Yeah, they live in 405."

My eyes widened at the answer. He looks at me, obviously knowing that something is afoot in my weird mind.

"Mr. and Mrs. Hidi? Those are your grandparents?" He shakes his head and parts his lips, almost as if he was wanting to speak, but didn't. We reach the bottom floor and start to make our way towards the lobby entrance. We walk side by side, silent, when I feel pressure on my arm. His hand is wrapped perfectly around my bicep. We stop and stare into each other's eyes, his dark, mine golden. His touch was as warm as the air around us, my heart started beating in my throat, making it hard to swallow.

He immediately retracts his arm, knowing that the physical contact made me uncomfortable. I don't think he understood that it made me uncomfortable, because it made me comfortable. He clears his throat one more time, trying to almost apologize without having to say anything.

"You never told me where you're going," he says with shy eyes, now looking at the tiled floor.

"Castino's," I reply without more information. A few seconds goes by, unmoved, I look at him. "My key broke in my lock, I can't get it out, and my friends didn't answer their door, so I'm kinda stuck and need a place to stay," I ramble before he cuts me off.

"I'll take you," he says digging his keys out of his pockets.

"Now why would I get in the car with someone I just met today."

He laughs, a beautiful dangerous laugh. "Now I know we didn't just meet today, Annie." Crap. I start racking my brain for the possible moment I may have told him my name, and I realize I hadn't. He remembered. He knew who I was.

"Wait, if you knew who I was, why didn't you say anything

at Jamie's?" I ask with pure curiosity.

"I didn't know at Jamie's, but you called me Mr. Myers in the elevator. And I put two and two together."

"My bad." I took a few seconds to think over what I had done. "Wait, how did you know I didn't just take it from the business card you gave me earlier?"

He looked at me with a smirk, knowing what he was doing to my mind. "It doesn't have my last name, silly." His smile grows as he fumbles with the keys now in his hand.

I look at the same tiles he was looking at just moments ago. "Well, don't I seem stupid now?"

He laughs again. Gosh, that laugh. "Not stupid, but I wouldn't call you observant either."

We started walking towards the lobby exit again, more like strolling, we were in no rush. I try to keep my giggles and creeping smiles hidden, but by the time we reached his car, it didn't seem to matter anymore.

Once we reach the doors, he looks at me again. "So a ride?"

I would never want to get into the Jordan Myers car, or so I thought. I can't tell if I accepted the offer purely because gas prices are no joke, or I accepted because I wanted to continue the conversation. Either way, I was getting in Mr. Myers car on my own terms.

We reach the visitors parking lot of my apartment complex I realize I'm burning up in the eighty degree summer night. I hadn't taken my sweatshirt off from the hours at Russ's. I take off the hoodie, trying to not mess up my freshly curled hair. I had taken out my messy bun approximately twenty minutes into being in the sixty-six degree apartment in hopes to warm me some. Why did I care if my hair got messed up? I suddenly realize I'm not wearing makeup either. I pinch my arm lightly as if to punish myself. Getting in Jordan Myers car is not a special occasion. I only wear makeup for special occasions.

He nods in the direction of a 2019 Ford Fusion deep red.

"Wow, nice car," I say, a little shell shocked. He had done well enough to own a car from the current year.

"Thanks?" He says with a touch of inflection. I start to take my left hand and raise it from my side to open the door, but he beats me to it. He opens the door and waits till I'm in the car, comfortable in the leather seats.

"Thank you… you know for the ride."

He gives me a nod that says, "No problem" and I wait for him to come around to the driver's side. He opens the back driver's side door and throws a backpack in; I hadn't noticed he was wearing it until just now, he must have only been wearing it on one shoulder. He shuts the door and walks to the driver's side. I'm in awe that he only had to shut it once, and it stayed shut. He gets in and turns the ignition on while putting on his seatbelt.

"Buckle up," he says with a grin.

"Thank you for taking me, I don't mean for you to go out of the way for me." He looks at me and then back at the rear windshield. He puts his arm on my headrest and looks behind us as we start backing up, despite the backup camera already installed in the car.

"It's really not out of the way." He says that, but it feels like it was said only to make me feel better about it. I hear him say more words, but I'm hyper focused on how close he is to me right now. My breath quickens and heartbeat races, but I hope he doesn't notice. "Business deals make you blush, Annie?" I feel my face, he's right I am blushing. Once I notice my face feels like it's on fire, which only causes me to become more red.

"Sorry, I wasn't paying attention. What were you saying?"

He briefly shakes his head as he puts the car in drive.

"Doesn't matter, not very interesting anyway."

I refocus my attention to the glove box, and it stays there the entire ride. I cannot get into this right now. I have school and work, and Russ and Laura. Feelings do not belong in my mind, at least not these feelings. Are they even considered that? It's only been a day, but it feels like he never disappeared after graduation night.

We drove fifteen minutes in silence to Castino's. It felt like eternity. We pull into the parking lot, and make our way around to the back entrance. My heart drops and I get concerned.

"You aren't going to kill me, are you?" He laughs for what feels like forever. I think I could get used to that laugh. He doesn't say no, he simply ignores my concern. We pull into a spot that says 'Employee's only'.

Without thinking, I say, "These spots are for employees, only," pointing at the obvious sign in front of us.

"I know." He puts the car in park and turns off the ignition. He works here? How can someone work at a hotel and make enough to buy this car? I leave the thoughts unanswered. He grabbed his backpack from the rear seat and before I was even fully unbuckled, he came over to my side and opened the door for me. I was an independent woman, but I have to admit I liked having him open my door.

I take the sweatshirt from my lap and slowly get up and out of the car. I can feel the heat rush to my face again. I wish I wasn't so pale; it makes it surprisingly obvious when I get flustered. I wish I had his skin tone, perfectly tanned, like he had been by the poolside all summer long. Maybe he's the hotel's pool boy? It explains the parking and the tan. He shuts the door behind me and we make our way to the only visible door that also states

'Employee's Only'. He swipes a keycard that makes the door's keypad light up green. Opening the door as I duck under his arm holding it in place. I start walking through the hallway, when he starts pacing ahead of me. He seems to know where to go.

At the end of what seems like a very long hallway, we turn left, and enter a room that says 'Management only'. Management, the car, the business card. It all made sense.

"You're the manager of Castino's?"

He looks at me with one raised eyebrow. "Well, you sure know how to wound a heart. You weren't listening in the car?"

I shake my head, embarrassed, and look at the similar tiles that we had seen at the apartment complex.

"I bought this place a month back, the guy sold it for super cheap just to get at his dad apparently." Owner? He was the owner of Castino's?

I looked back up to him, and pushed the one strand of black hair that hung in my face. Our eyes met again. Except this time, it looked like he was looking at mine with just as much concentration that I had been looking at his eyes with.

I break the silence that went on for a few seconds, maybe more. "How on earth did you afford to buy a business at twenty-three?" He breaks my gaze, and sits in a red desk chair while gesturing to a black swivel chair across from the wooden desk. Sitting at the opposite end of the desk made me feel like I had gotten in trouble, and was sitting in the principal's office.

"Just turned twenty-three actually, and I took out a loan, you know… from the bank? Plus, I used all the money I saved from previous work for any upfront costs."

"Wow, all yours." I am still in shock.

"All mine," Jordan said with definity gesturing with his arms out wide looking towards the ceiling..

Chapter 2

Castino's

Jordan fixed me up with a really nice room, free of charge. I was more than grateful. It meant that I didn't have to take out any savings. I could barely afford rent, and mainly lived off of my savings account I built throughout high school. It made me wonder if I could've bought Castino's with my savings instead of what I'm doing with it now, I was a very financially savvy person, but always found myself with less than I expected.

I was led to the elevator with Jordan walking a few paces in front of me.

"Third floor, just to the right," he says as he pushes the up arrow.

"Thank you again, it really means a lot." And it did. I held onto my savings for a reason. I never want to be in the same position that I've seen other people go through before. I wanted, *needed* a backup. The elevator doors opened, and Jordan leaned in and pressed the third floor button and backed into the first floor hallway.

"Goodnight," Jordan said tiredly. He took one hand out of his pockets and waved me off, and I did the same. I tucked my head to my chin as the doors close and realize I didn't say goodnight back. This man just let me stay at *his* hotel for free and I couldn't even give him the respect of a response. What is wrong with me?

When I reached the third floor, I got off and looked around. The signs hanging from the ceiling indicated the ice machine and vending were to my left. I decided to make a pit stop there first. I hadn't realized until reading the sign that I was thirsty, morbidly thirsty. I turn left and then right to the end of the hall to a little room that contains exactly what the sign said. The ice and vending machines were quite loud, but not nearly as loud as the elevator back home, so the sound didn't bother me. I stick the only dollar bill crumpled beyond belief. I use the side of the machine and go back and forth until it is straight enough that the machine could possibly take it. I put the bill into the drink machine and press on the Diet Coke option, even though I know I should be getting water. The drink dispenses, and when I bend over to grab it, I hear a crowd of people heading towards the area I'm in. My worst nightmare after the day I have had, people.

I peak my head out and see a group of guys aged twenty to thirty head my way. I start to panic so I grab my drink and start heading out the way I came, but it's too late.

"Woo! We've got a live one! What's your name, little thing?" Obviously drunk. I try to push past the men, I don't utter a word or sound. I ignore the comment. I'm not little; in fact, I'm around 5'8, which is considered pretty tall compared to who I went to high school with. After trying to push past them one of them grabs my arm, and asks me what the rush is I let out a gasp of distain and fight to pull my arm out of his grip, but with every move it becomes tighter and tighter. The other guys were laughing around him. He seemed to be their 'leader' of sorts, the one that called the shots. I feel myself shrinking, not physically, but in every other way possible. How could this day get any worse for me?

I broke my arm free. This wasn't like when Jordan grabbed

my arm; that was full of concern and trust, this was not that. I tried again to move past them, but there were too many. Twenty? Fifteen? Probably not that many in reality, but it sure felt like it was more than I could fight off.

Suddenly I hear a voice come from behind them. "All right guys, go back to your rooms, leave the girl alone." The voice is soft, but stern, as if it were a threat of what the mysterious voice would do if they didn't obey. No matter what, I'm very grateful that I have been saved. At least I hope I was being saved.

The guys start backing up, murmuring about what a buzzkill this person was.

I look up, only now realizing that I had a single tear going down my hot cheek, and my eyes were welling with more.

"I'm sorry, I came as soon as I saw them. They're here for a bachelor party. They were obviously wasted." It was Jordan. He was looking down the hall, making sure they actually went to their rooms. I start wiping my face looking at my hand noticing the back of it was now wet, when he looks back at me.

"Woah, hey, are you ok?" Suddenly his arms are around me. I didn't know how to react, but I sunk in and let the tears flow. I had been in situations like that before, but I felt so hopeless that time. He rests his head on the top of mine and just lets me cry. It felt humiliating when I let go, but felt so comfortable and healing in the moment. *He protected me.* He barely knows who I am, and he protected me. Maybe he was just that type of guy now, maybe he would have done that for any other girl in that situation.

I catch my breath from the lack of oxygen from crying. "I…I'm sorry it's just… they were… how did you?" I didn't finish my sentence.

"The best part of owning this place is the cameras that come with it." He points to the black security camera in the corner opposite to me in the small room. It was one of those cameras that you weren't sure was an actual camera.

"Oh… I didn't know those were there." I say, still shaking. I didn't know they were there, but boy was I grateful they were.

He shakes his head. "It's eleven o'clock and you're having a Diet Coke? He was trying to lighten the mood. Truth be told, that's why I was looking at this camera to begin with. I was amazed that you were getting Diet Coke instead of water."

I giggled and wiped the wetness off of my face, which had seemed to cool a few degrees. "Listen, I have a diet coke wherever I go. I just didn't get the chance to grab one from my place before I was whisked away by a stranger to a hotel in the middle of nowhere. I figure if you were going to kill me in my sleep, I may as well be happy beforehand." Once I finish speaking, I giggle again. His face seems to soften just a little, but I try not to read too much into it.

"Let me walk you to your room. I want to make sure those guys aren't waiting."

I nod, even though I could stay here watching him forever. We start walking and I realize I keep having the thoughts that aren't allowed. The thoughts that make me like the boy who once teased me so much in eighth grade. Was it petty of me to hold a grudge this long? I mean without Jordan I wouldn't have become best friends with Russ. I try to shake myself out of it, but I realize there is no use. I can tolerate Jordan Myers. I may even like Jordan Myers.

We reach my door, Number 308, and I swipe my keycard to open the door wait for the indicator light to change from red to green, and then push down on the handle. I stand in the doorframe and turn around, holding the door open with just my back. Jordan stood just a few feet away from me. We sat there staring before I finally waved just as we did on the original elevator ride up here. He waved back with that stupid smirk.

I shut my door unwillingly, but I know I need sleep, it's almost midnight. I stay with my head against the door and sigh it was one of those moments where dramatic music plays in your head. It has been a day, and I didn't realize how exhausted I was until just now whenI set my very few things on the chair in the living area. This was a nice room, almost nicer than my apartment. I felt guilty not paying for it, but accepted the gesture I was too tired to go back down and ask Jordan to move me to a smaller room. I make my way towards the bedroom when I realize I'm still in my jeans and Hard Rock shirt from earlier. It wasn't the most comfortable thing to be sleeping in, but it would have to do. I shift my pull-on sneakers off my feet, take off my pizza socks and set them on the ground next to the bed. I shift into the bed, plug my phone in for the night and shut my eyes.

Before I know it, morning had arrived. I look at my phone and it's almost nine thirty. I rarely sleep in this late, at least I rarely sleep this late on a weekday. I stretch the type of stretch that makes noises come out of you involuntarily when I hear a knock at the door. I hadn't even finished my morning stretching before I was interrupted. I had I feeling I knew who it was.

Without thinking, I head over to the door, rubbing my eyes with the back of my fists so they adjust to the light quicker all it does is create flashes of light in my vision and disorient me temporarily. I open the door yawning, without a care in the world.

"Well, looks like someone slept well."

I immediately drop my hands and force the yawn to halt. Jordan is standing in front of me in a suit that only one could dream of. The light blue long sleeved shirt matched perfectly with the black sports coat, tie and slacks he had with it. I look down and notice the ensemble is paired with fine leather dress shoes the perfect shade of brown. His hands were in his pockets, they were always in his pockets. It made it seem like he was a shy kid who didn't know what to do with them during conversation.

After taking my gaze from the suit I realize how I must look. My hair tangled from rolling in my sleep, my eyes with horrendous bags, and maybe even drool covered lips. I try to take the focus off me.

"I did, thank you again for the room. You didn't have to put me in such a nice one, I can sleep anywhere. You could've given me keys to the janitor closet and all would have been well." I'm doing my best to control my hair while speaking, slowly raking my fingers through my tangled curls, without it being too noticeable.

He laughs and combines it with an upward smile. "I wouldn't have put you in the closet, Annie. Don't flatter yourself either, it was the only room left."

My head snaps back into reality. What I thought was flirtation throughout the previous night was simply him doing a favor. He didn't want anything in return, not even me.

"There's continental breakfast downstairs. It closes in thirty minutes; I didn't want you to miss out." Even though he doesn't know me as well as he used to, he obviously knows the way to this girl's heart is food. Specifically breakfast food.

I eagerly nod my head and say, "Be down in five."

He shakes his head and starts walking away. I let the door close as I walked towards the bed. I slip on my socks and shoes from the night before and grab my things. I even put my sweatshirt back on, even though it was warm inside.

I make my way out the door and towards the elevator where

I see Jordan standing.

"I didn't want you to get lost, you look like someone who might." He chuckles and I stick my tongue out at him, mocking his smile. I try to remember that this was just a one time thing, if I stop it now I won't get too attached.

He pushes the down arrow, and we slowly enter along with another group of people, obviously heading towards breakfast as well. The crowd rushes out as the doors open to the packed first floor. I feel a hand touch the small of my back. I tense while trying to keep my cool. Once the rest of the group on the elevator has left, and the hand remained, I realized who it was. Jordan guides me with his hand to the buffet. It was beautiful. You may catch me saying that about any type of food, but breakfast was my favorite.

Once we arrive in the breakfast area, his hand leaves my back. Leaving it cold and empty. We both grab plates and make our way through the line. I stack my plate high with eggs, sausage, bacon, potatoes, and waffles. He grabs a blueberry muffin and apple juice and waits for me. He looks with that smirk towards my plate and laughs to himself.

"What! Breakfast is the most important meal of the day."

He shakes his head, still laughing at what I had just said. We sit across from each other at the only available table in the lobby. He picks at his blueberry muffin and sips his apple juice, while I dig in. No wonder he has that figure. He barely eats.

Jordan finishes off his plate and watches me scarf down the rest. "Locksmith is coming to your place at 11. It's all paid for."

I look up from my plate in awe. "You didn't have to do that, I'll pay you back, please," I say forcefully. If I made it a business arrangement it felt less awkward.

"He's an old friend, so I got a good deal, don't worry about it.”

I protest some more but know it won't get me anywhere. I'm learning he has become just as stubborn as I am. Eventually I gave up. Once my plate was finished, he took it and walked across the lobby and set it on top of the stack already made on the trash can.

He sat in front of me and we just talked. We talked like we never hated each other, like he didn't make me hate school. In fact, it felt like the opposite, it felt like I was talking to someone I liked. That I had been best friend with and simply lost connection to. It felt like I had been having this conversation for years.

"What's the suit for?" I ask, gesturing towards the jacket that is laid on his shoulders.

"Oh, I've got a few meetings this afternoon, so I just got ready now instead of later." I realize we look so different, and we must have gotten stared at throughout breakfast. Here is this man in a suit, dirty blonde hair combed back, smells amazing, next to this girl. I immediately felt out of place. My oversized sweatshirt, and jeans, with a head of messy hair, suddenly making me feel so vulnerable.

"Are you excited for the meeting?" I knew people are rarely excited for business meetings. I grew up in a house with two working parents who barely saw the light of day because of how many meetings they were in, but I still asked the question.

"Actually, not really. It's a meeting with the city talking about licenses and all that." He made a gagging gesture, which made me chuckle.

"I know way too much about that, I'm sorry. Hopefully it goes your way though." Those were the meetings my parents despised. They owned a business together, and they hated having to pull focus from the actual work to talk about legalities. I had told him about what my parents did earlier in the conversation.

"So…" He hesitated. "If your parents both own a business, what are you doing in that apartment?" This is a question I get asked frequently. My parents were not well-off, but they were definitely comfortable with their finances, however I've never accepted a penny from them, even though they've offered. I reply the same way I always have, except this time I feel more defensive.

"I'm twenty-three. I don't need my parents' money, I've got savings, and a job, and I don't need a dime." I realize how I came across. It was significantly more aggressive than intended. He looks at me with a shocked face. I had been criticized my whole life about how I had these parents who could do whatever, and I didn't want that as an adult.

"I'm sorry…I didn't mean it that…"

I cut him off. "I know, I'm sorry, I've just been getting this question since I moved out and there comes a point where I'm a little tired of it." That was true, but my reaction wasn't due to tiredness of a question, it was who the question came from.

The lobby had cleared out. By now it was well past 10.

"It's 10:40. We should get going."

I nod, knowing that I hurt his feelings. I hand him the keys, and he hands them off to the receptionist.

"Thanks, Kira," he says. That must be her name.

I start walking outside. He promptly catches up to me and reminds me he parked out back. Rather than going through the lobby, we walk around the building, in complete silence.

I thought to myself. "You ruined it, you could've had a shot at having a friend other than Russ and Laura, and you went and did what you do."

We reach his car, I wait for him to open the door for me, and realize he's already on the other side sliding in. My heart aches a little. He backs up, hand on the back of my headrest like before, but I keep my gaze out the window. This time I turn my face towards the window so I'm not as close to him as before.

We arrive at my complex, and he pulls to my building.

"We're here." The way he spoke felt different than the previous day, even just the previous hour. It was short and matter-of-fact, rather than soft. I get out of the car and face my building, shutting the passenger door behind me. I hear his car drive off, and I turn around and wave. I receive no wave back. I slowly start walking into the lobby. I decided to take the stairs. I could use the minute to unwind.

When I reach the door that says 'Floor 2'. I open it and enter my hallway. I lived in 201, which was directly to my left. I start my way over there and notice a man crouching near my door handle. It must be the locksmith. I made my way over to my apartment, a little quicker than I would normally. I figured I should probably introduce myself to the man who was about to have access to my apartment.

"Hi, I'm Anna, are you the locksmith?" I put my hand out and prepare for a handshake, but the locksmith doesn't look up.

"Yep, name's Jace, Jace Treemont."

Jace Treemont was not what I would expect from a locksmith. He seemed well put together, was in amazing shape, but rugged at the same time. It looked as though he got paid to look the way he looks, and if he doesn't, he definitely should be.

Jace Treemont… it sounded familiar, but I knew that if this was someone I once knew in the small town of Wallace, that I would already know everything about him.

"Jace, do I know you somewhere? Have we met before?"

The question was eating at me, I knew everyone and everything, except apparently who owns the hotels across town.

"I don't think we've ever met before. I work for Jordan at the hotel across town. You ever been?"

It clicked. I saw his name on the employee roster sitting on Jordans desk in the management office. He sent one of his employees fifteen minutes out, to take a key out of my door handle.

"Oh! That's how I recognize the name, I just stayed there last night. Due to the… you know… key stuck in my handle."

He huffs as if I had said something funny, it wasn't quite a full laugh, but it wasn't nothing.

"Thank you again for doing this. I know Jordan said he was going to pay you, but I would really like to, if you don't mind." My voice becomes shy as the words come out of my mouth. My lips thin into a straight line, waiting for a response. I didn't realize I had been smiling, it almost felt forceful to contain my mouth. I was always happy, nothing to complain about; having to not show it was something that I didn't realize was difficult until just now.

"Boss man will kill me if I accept your money, he told me you would pull something like this, called me just before you showed up." Jordan must have called him while he pulled away. He pulls out a pair of pliers and looks up at me, letting his words trail off as he pulls the end of the key from the handle without almost any effort. "Do you have any spare keys? I'll make a copy of the broken one, but you'll need one until then."

Do I own any spare keys? I must, right? If I do, they're upstairs with Russ and Laura, so I won't be able to get it until they both come back from work.

"Yes, I do." I tell a half truth. I'm sure I do, I just have no clue where it is, or who has it, which probably isn't the safest, but I didn't want to tell a total stranger that I had lost it. I give a smile for reassurance, hoping he doesn't know that I have no clue where that small gold key is.

"Alrighty then, I'll unlock the door for you, and you can grab anything you need, including your spare key, and then I'll be on my way," he says, starting to stand up from his once knelt position.

"That's great. I appreciate it." I smile once more and watch him unlock my door with some kind of pick. Once he's fully standing, I realize he's just as tall and built as Jordan. Same rock-solid jawline and built arms. Wow, who knew to find attractive men, all I had to do was drive fifteen minutes east?

He holds the door for me as I enter my apartment. I handed him the top of my broken key, while he played with the other half in his left hand.

"I'll make a copy of this for you and bring it back once it's ready, should only take a day or two." He waves the top of the key in the air to say goodbye.

I shout a little thank you as he makes his way to the elevator. Once I turn back into my apartment, I realize I am so glad I cleaned yesterday. He definitely would have made me pick up the key at Castino's if he saw the pig stye that once was.

I take a seat on the couch, and start taking my phone out of my pocket. 20%. 20%? How is my phone's battery low? I realize that my plug must not have been fully connected to the outlet last night, meaning it didn't charge. I sigh to myself, opening my satchel where I put my phone charger this morning. I move around the other items in my bag to locate the cord and plug, but find nothing. All that's there is gum, my wallet, and a stray hair tie or two.

"Crap." I say with disdain. Last night I would have been so excited to go back, but after this morning I'm not sure that I want to. My phone buzzes and reminds me of the low battery warning. I yell at myself for not having multiple chargers, but I was cheap and didn't find it necessary at the time.

I set my phone on the couch cushion next to me, and start to stand up. I was supposed to go into the city to grab a few other things anyway. I look at my list hanging on the stainless steel fridge and decide I should go. I study the list as I tear the paper from the magnet. Deodorant, toothpaste, command strips, hair tics, and now phone charger and plug. I study the list several more times, but get stuck on the second line. Deodorant. I already had deodorant, but ever since that night at the dance I always made sure I had plenty of stock. Who knew toiletries could give such problems. I drop the list to my side and gather my things, and start making my way towards the door. I realize how I look as I pass the mirror hanging by my front door. Usually, I would pay no mind to it, I didn't care. Something made me turn on my heels and set my things back down. I should shower, and change.

I make my way towards the bathroom and remove all my clothing with no care. I turn on the shower, but no water flows just a few cold drops fall into my outstretched palm. I try the handle a few more times, and then the sink to confirm. I have no running water. What the heck? I go back to my room and put on fresh clothing. I check my apartment's app on my phone, still dying.

"My bills have been paid." I say softly. That can't be the problem. I'm about to call maintenance, when I see I have 3 unread emails. One is the apartment's newsletter; I never read those. They were mainly filled with warnings for parents to keep their kids together, and rules of the complex. I open it despite not wanting to read through the slurry of unhelpful news. The bottom of the email is filled with bright bold letters. 'Reminder, water will be shut off July 23rd from 11:30-1 for Maintenance'. Of course. The few hours I'm home, I have no running water.

I slap some deodorant on as I read through the other two emails. One is from Hobby Lobby, it's the monthly coupons I get that no one knows about. The other from someone I don't recognize. The email is Kira@CHotel.com.

Hi Anna,
While housekeeping was cleaning your room, we found a phone charging cord and outlet. We will keep it up front for you to pick up anytime today at your earliest convenience.
Hope you had a nice stay!
Kira

Would it look bad if I didn't reply, but also didn't show up? I decided to be a better person and reply.

Hi Kira!
Thanks for the heads up, I'm actually going into the city for a few other things, and will just pick up another one there. Thanks Again!
Anna

I hope I didn't come off harsh or ungrateful, but there was no way I was going back to that hotel. May as well cut things off now rather than wait until I'm fully invested. Once I'm finished freshening up, I brush out my day-old curls and call it good, they definitely weren't perfect and had a piece hanging out from the edge that was driving me nuts, but it was just a grocery store trip.

I would survive. I start heading out the door when I stop myself and look back in the bathroom mirror. I grab and eyelash curler and squeeze it against both sets of eyelashes a few times and apply my two-year-old mascara, I know it's well past expired by the clumping and smell, but it was a gift, and it would take a lot for me to buy makeup. It's not supermodel-pretty, but I looked somewhat more alive now. I start my way back towards the door and wonder why I did that. Since when is Walmart makeup worthy?

I ignore the thought and head out the door. I leave it unlocked. Usually this would be dangerous, but the only criminals we have here are typically apprehended very quickly since the police don't get many thrills. I didn't have the energy to go talk to Russ and Laura right now, I needed some time alone. I decide to take the elevator at the end of the hallway and press the down arrow instead of the up. The doors immediately open and I step inside. I press 1 and the doors creak close and the elevator starts to move, as always coming to an abrupt halt once it reaches its destination.

I took a big breath before exiting the elevator. I started having an all too familiar feeling, the type of feeling you get after breaking up with someone you have been with for only 3 months. I was attached. I tried to convince myself that I was attached to the idea of someone treating me the way Jordan treated me that night, being taken care of, not having to worry about anything more than getting up.

I make my way to my assigned parking spot and unlock my car, although I'm pretty sure it doesn't lock anymore, but I do it to feel a little better, I can't have both my apartment and car not locking. I force the driver's side open and shut the door a few times till it sticks. I envy Jordan's car and the way it smoothly shuts without an issue. I turn the rattling ignition on, while I blast the 90s and early 00s hits, singing along, I'm pretty sure if anyone could hear me they would roll up their windows and start heading in the opposite direction. I drive for about twenty minutes south before I reach where I need to be. The parking lot was always full since this was the only Walmart for a few towns that surround it. I make my way to an open parking spot and start towards the store, same brown satchel that I had at Josie's. The leather was starting to crack from the wear and tear it has endured over the years.

I grab all of my list, along with a premade salad to have for lunch, the energy I once had is slowly fading. I wish that I hadn't run into Jordan at the supermarket, and I wish that I didn't let myself get into the car with him last night. I head over to self-checkout and start scanning. I reach the end and the last item is the phone cord and outlet. I sit for a minute contemplating, and decide not to scan the cord and outlet. I finish up and check my bank account to ensure I have the needed $23.97 I do, I have plenty, but I still check every time. I slip my card out of my pocket and slide it into the machine, press a few buttons and then remove. I slide the card back into my pocket, but immediately go back and put it in its rightful place in my wallet. I see the business card Jordan gave me. I realized I hadn't read it thoroughly. The crumpled blue edges fit nicely into my hand, and I see he was right, his last name isn't on here, just Castino's, a few phone numbers and an email.

I take out my phone and dial the first number I see, all of this without taking a minute to think. I slide my phone up to my ear, gather my receipt and two plastic bags and head out to my car. The other side rings for what feels like hours. Finally, a voice picks up.

"Jordan Myers, Castino's, how can I help you?"

I breathe for a minute to myself while Jordan repeats himself on the other line. I notice I haven't said anything, I sound like such a creep. I find myself overwhelmed with feeling, and tears almost start to well into my eyes, but I don't let them fall to my warm cheeks. My energy is slowly returning, and so is a stomachache.

"Hi, it's…"

"Annie, I was hoping you would call. Did you decide I owe you that shirt after all?"

I pause again, he doesn't hate me. What's even worse is that I don't hate him.

"No, you would find a way to get the wrong one anyway. I got an email from Kira, she said something about a phone cord?"

I pack my things into my car and force my door close as I get into the hot fabric seat beneath me. I didn't call him about the phone cord. I don't know why I called him, I just did.

"Oh yeah, it's just hanging out at the front desk. I can keep it for you." He hesitates. "Or I can swing by tonight and drop it off…"

Not happening, I will not let him see the inside of my apartment. I will not let him know my apartment number. I realize he already does, since he sent the locksmith there this morning. Either way, this is not a good idea.

"Hello?" I realized once again my tongue was tied. I hadn't spoken.

"That's ok, I'll come pick it up. I can be there in around one thirty?"

Without any breath for interruption, he says, "Perfect, I'll see you here."

It's a little past twelve fifty by the time I make my way across the city and back in town to Castino's. I walk in the front doors. It seems so much brighter and welcoming than when I snuck through the back last night. I see Kira wave me down, as if we have known each other for years.

"Anna! Hey! Jordan's in his office, I'll let him know you're here," she says with a little too much enthusiasm.

"No, that's ok, I'm just here for a phone charger. I don't want to bother him. I know he has meetings." I wanted to, but I knew it would only cause more problems down the line if I let myself continue whatever this was.

She lets out a sigh of disappointment, like what I said just crushed her inside. "Ok no problem, here you go." She opens the drawer that sits at her waist. She's tiny, no taller than 5'4, with long blonde hair that reaches the end of her ribcage. She pulls out the cord and outlet and slides them across the counter and pats them. I snag them and start turning around.

"Annie, wait!" It's that voice, the voice that I despise, but love hearing. I turn around, and Jordan is within a foot of me.

I have to lean my head back to meet his eyes, we both realize at the same time how close we are and scoot a few inches in the opposite direction. I drop my gaze to the floor, and he scratches the back of his head. My stomachache gets worse, and I realize if we hadn't walked a few paces backwards, we would be touching noses.

"Um, I thought we could get lunch while you're here. We could go to the diner across the street, or somewhere else." He desperately looks at Kira, who I notice is giving him a thumbs up, but puts her hands down swiftly when I catch her.

"Actually, I bought a salad already so I'm OK. Thanks though, maybe another time." That was a hard sentence. I really wanted to go, but I couldn't let this man infiltrate my life. He had already given me a hotel room, a locksmith, what's next? I didn't want to find out.

He takes the hand scratching his nape and stuffs it into the pockets of his slacks. He gives the saddest and most shallow nod I have ever seen. His eyes, sad in demeanor, look towards the ground. I couldn't take it anymore.

"I mean, if you have a fridge I can stick it in, I can just eat it later."

His eyes light up and meet mine again. His deep, beautifully brown eyes. "Sure, where is it? I'll grab it for you and stick it in my office." Along with his eyes, Kira's light up too. Their plan had worked, and I fell victim to the man I once hated.

"No, I'll grab it myself, and meet you back here." He starts to protest, but I stand my ground. I did not want him to see my car.

I come back a minute or two later with salad in hand and giving myself a minute to breathe at my car door. He touches the small of my back and sends an electric shock throughout my entire body. Why was it so easy for him to fluster me? Why did I feel this way when he was near me? I wave to Kira as we make our way to his all-too-familiar office. Once there, he removes the hand and grabs the salad, which I didn't realize I was holding onto tight enough to make my knuckles white. I sit in the chair while he makes his way to the only color in the room and sits in it. He spins the red chair to what I assume is a mini fridge under his desk. I watch his every move, his hands around the fridge, opening the door, sliding the Chicken BLT salad in. I audibly gasp. My eyes widen, I realize what just happened. Jordan Myers just literally took my breath away, and all it took was a fridge and a salad.

"You ready?" He asks me, with the smirk that untangles me.

He obviously heard my unfiltered gasp earlier. I nod, starting to feel the heat rush to my cheeks, and I hope he doesn't point them out. "Let's go then. Is the diner ok?"

All I can do is nod. I fear what will happen if I speak. I'm glad he decides to choose where we will eat, because right now I can't remember my name, birthday, or social security number. He takes his hand out from the pockets they were once in and reaches towards me. I grab on as he pulls me to his level, or, in our case, six inches below the top of his head. We're close, closer than we were in the lobby, closer than in the few car rides we had been on, closer than I wanted to be. We sat there, staring at each other, neither of us making any sudden movements. Neither of us dropped our gaze. The only thing that interrupts us is a knock at the door. Jordan's eyes darted over and opened the door quickly, leaving both of us out of breath, as if we had just ran a marathon.

It's Jace. Once the door is open, he darts his eyes in between both of us and starts looking a little flushed, like he had just walked in on something. He had, but we couldn't let him know that.

"Sorry, didn't mean to interrupt anything. I heard you were here," he gestures towards me, "so I brought you your key." It wasn't even one fifteen yet, he must've done it as soon as he got back from my apartment.

He plops the shiny gold metal into my hand, and tilts his hat covering his gorgeous auburn hair. He walks away, just as fast as he came. I clutch the key in my hand and stuff it in my satchel, the threads of which are breaking and fraying, but that would have to wait until August 15th, my birthday.

"After you." A voice interrupts my mind. He's always interrupting my thoughts, but I don't know if that's a good or bad thing. He does it again, guiding me by the small of my back out of his office door and towards the lobby entrance. Once we reach the elevators before the actual lobby, I feel his hand drop, no longer feeling his touch.

I shiver, almost as if his hand was the only thing keeping me warm, even though it was eighty-five degrees out. Without his touch it felt freezing.

"Are you ok with walking?" His voice low and soft, as if he didn't want anyone else to hear, as if this was a private conversation.

"Yeah, let's go." Jordan awkwardly gestures towards the obvious automatic doors at the entrance as if I didn't come in them minutes prior.

We make our way through the lobby, keeping a distance between us, obviously at the fear that if we don't something will happen, and he obviously doesn't want that. He's shut off, and keeps his hands in his pockets around me; he has no desire to do anything. The only time they come out, is to guide me somewhere, and then they slip right back in.

All I can think about is holding those hands. I want to hold those hands. I keep myself in check. I can't do this right now, I don't have time for it. We pass Kira and she looks as happy as ever watching us walk out. We make our way through the parking lot still keeping at least a couple of feet in between us, trying not to waiver from the path we had created for ourselves. I try not to look at my car. I don't want to give that away quite yet. Once we reach the sidewalk we stand in silence, waiting for the little white guy to appear on the screen across from us, indicating it was safe to cross.

Loo Ann's was a diner that had been here forever. Castino's and the diner were right across from each other both on corners of streets parallel to one another. I'm in my head more than usual, so I focus all of my attention on the red hand across from us, not saying a word. It turns white, and we start making our way across. No physical contact. We make it across, just in time for the countdown to end. It was a long enough countdown that we should have made it before then, but we were in no rush once again.

"Two, please," he says, raising his hand showing the number to the hostess.

"Follow me." She sounds tired, overworked. I feel bad. I used to work in the service industry; I remember the lunch rush and the rude customers. I'm so glad I was out of it. I slide into the booth we were guided to, and Jordan slides to the chair across from me. Still without a single word we look at the menus and occasionally look up and over to see the other person staring. I don't need to look at the menu, I've gotten the same thing since I was a kid, grilled cheese and tomato soup, no matter the time of year.

Finally, we're greeted by our waitress, who breaks the awkward tension that is happening right now.

"Can I get you started with some drinks? We've got lemonades, Coke products, and a few select beers."

"Water for me." Of course he gets water. I don't think that man has seen an ounce of soda. In fact, I don't remember ever seeing him drink soda, even when we were kids.

"Diet Coke for me," I say with a big smile, knowing what is about to come my way.

"Thank you," he says, trying to hide his laugh. "Diet Coke huh? When's the last time you had water?" He didn't need to know the real answer to that question.

People teased me about this all the time, so I replied with something somewhat rehearsed. "Did you know water is the main ingredient? I'm plenty hydrated."

He links his fingers in front of him, elbows on the standard dining table and laughs. I feel like I haven't heard it in years. I've been craving it, wanting to hear that laugh. I smile and laugh back. I would do anything to hear that laugh.

Our laughter is interrupted by my phone ringing. It's Russ. It's already one thirty. I've never missed a call from him on his break. I turn my phone over and silence it. I feel guilty, but I think I would feel worse if I wasted any time that I had with the man sitting across from me. I set my hands interlocked in my lap and looked over.

"Hey, I'm sorry about this morning. I didn't mean to be so harsh about what I said." He meets my gaze. "I just…Everyone thinks that my parents hand me everything, and I hate it. I work really hard, I go to school, I work weekends, I worked all throughout high school. It just seems unfair is all."

His eyes drop. "I shouldn't have pried. It was my fault, I shouldn't have brought it up." His voice is sincere. It makes my heart jump. I start getting butterflies in my stomach, something I haven't felt in years. I wonder if that was the stomachache I had felt earlier.

We order our food and eat slowly once it arrives. He taunts my grilled cheese compared to his steak, and I get a few refills of my Diet Coke, him shaking his head with every single one.

"I've got to go." He signals our waitress for the check. "It's two thirty and my meeting with the city is at three."

My heart sinks. I don't want this to end, I don't want any of this to end. "Ok, no problem. Hey, good luck with them." Our waitress sets the check down. "Oh, this was supposed to be separate." I say with the utmost confidence.

"No, I've got it." Woah. I don't know why, but those four

words really did me in. I was too stunned to protest, by the time I had realized that he was paying for my meal the waitress had already left with his card.

I smile and put up no fight as he slides the card into the slot and hands it back to the waitress. She comes back moments later and he takes the receipt and gives her a 20% tip. A gentleman. Unfortunately, I have a rule with all men. If they don't leave a tip, they will never see me again. I'm so relieved to know I can see him again. Although unfortunately for me, I think I would have broken that rule if it came down to it.

We make our way back to the hotel. I get in my car as he watches with a concerned look on his face.

"It still runs, no need to worry." I smile playfully, hopefully easing his worries. I realized what I had done. I let him have another piece of me. I let him see my car and I didn't think twice about it. This was going to end in heartbreak. I knew who Jordan was deep down, and it wasn't something I wanted to experience again.

"OK, OK. Just don't do anything stupid. I'll text you tonight." He starts heading inside.

"How? You don't have my number!" I shout back.

He cups his hands to his face and walks backwards into the lobby. "No, but I do have a caller ID!" He's right, I'm an idiot. I called him today.

I drive back to my apartment in silence, no radio, no phone, complete silence. The only thing I can hear is my cheeks to my ears as I smile so loud. Uh oh. I'm falling. It's been two days and I'm falling hard.

Chapter 3

Waiting

I make my way up the elevator and into my apartment with my newly made key. I insert the key, holding my breath. It smoothes its way in and turns without any issues I lock and unlock it to make sure it works both directions. Once I make my way into my apartment I set my things down and hang my satchel on my brown, treelike coat rack. I sigh heavily, as if all the pressure has been lifted off my shoulders. I just don't know where the pressure was coming from. I yawn and realize I'm tired. I make my way towards the bedroom, rubbing my eyes with my balled fists, only to realize the mascara now taking over my pointer and thumb.

"Dangit." I move directions to the bathroom and take off the mascara and wash my hands free from it. "This is why I don't wear makeup." I grunt as I finish drying my hands on the light pink hand towel hanging from the crooked ring affixed to the wall.

I wander into my bedroom and change into comfier clothes. I get into black leggings and a large 'what's the word bird?' shirt. I plug my phone into my retrieved charger and finally close my eyes.

I woke up to pounding on my door. I realize it's almost six P.M. I slept for three hours. I rush to collect my thoughts and stumble through the hallway into the living room. I finally reach the door and open it. Russ and Laura are panting at my doorstep.

They both force their way in.

"What the heck, Anna! You didn't answer your phone at lunch! I thought you were dead!"

I spin on my heels and slump myself on the couch. "I was just with Jordan. Calm down."

They stop dead in their tracks.

"What?" Laura asks genuinely curious. Russ says nothing but just gives me a blank stare.

"Well just so we're clear, if you two weren't old people, none of that would have happened." I spilled everything: the key, the elevators, the hotel, the arms, the hands.

"You are not seriously blaming us right now for your poor life decisions," Russ says, almost too angrily.

"Poor life decision? What makes you think this was a poor life decision?"

He doesn't respond.

Laura stands from her place on the couch and drags Russ with her. "We just wanted to make sure you were ok. I'm…we're glad you are." Her voice comforts me. She knew Russ reacted poorly and wanted to make up for it.

Once they're gone, I sink back into the place I spent the last hour and a half. I realize I haven't eaten since lunch, and I didn't retrieve my salad from Jordan's fridge. I whip up a PB & J and grab a Diet Coke from my fridge and call it good. I watch whatever's on cable while I finish my 'meal'.

I remember I had done laundry the day before and had fresh clothes that needed to be put away. I pull them from the dryer, periodically checking my phone to see if Jordan has texted as he promised. Nothing, and it was getting late.

Once I finish folding and putting away my clothes, I take a shower, change and head to bed. I was upset with myself for being upset he hadn't texted. What did I expect? None of our encounters were dates, but I liked being around him. I wait until eleven P.M. and finally call it quits. I hate him again, but for a different reason. I hate him because he gives me butterflies, but I don't make him have the same reaction.

When I wake up, I check my phone again, and become disappointed once more. Nothing.

It's Friday morning, the last day to turn in my assignments for the week, so I get out my computer and get to work. I hadn't finished anything since the day I ran into him. I hadn't been able to focus enough. Lucky for me, I can focus now, knowing that feelings aren't reciprocated. I'm learning about children's literature. I have to send a video of myself reading a book to the professor. I pull out the only children's book I own. 'The Very Hungry Caterpillar' by Eric Carle. I read the designated time and submit the video. I looked awful, but I didn't care. It was refreshing to not care.

It's noon, but I'm not hungry, despite not having eaten today. I go to the fridge and pull out a bottle of water. Not my drink of choice, but maybe Jordan was right, I do need to drink more water. I down the bottle and threw it away in the trash can under my sink overflowing with Diet Coke and paper plates.

Tonight is Thai night at Russ and Laura's. I forgot to buy anything at the store on Wednesday, but I didn't want to have to see others for the third day in a row, so I scoured my fridge and freezer. I found some stir fry veggies and frozen egg rolls. Not really Thai food, but it would have to do. I wasn't going back, no matter what.

Time flies relatively quickly while I wait for it to be time to head upstairs. On Fridays we met at seven, but I was always gone by ten thirty. I grab all my things, stuff them in my satchel and carry the veggies and egg rolls in an old plastic bag, locking my door with my new key behind me. My phone buzzes. It's the text tone. I'm more hopeful that I should be. Still facing my door, I pull the phone out of my bag.

Hey it's Jace, Jace Treemont, the locksmith?

Hi Jace, how did you get my number lol

I'm not gonna lie, I stole it from Jordan's work phone, I wanted to ask if you wanted to do something next week.

I hesitated before answering. Letting the bubbles hang out on Jace's phone for a moment.

Sure, why not. I'm busy Wednesdays and Fridays, but any other day works.

I work those nights, how about tomorrow instead?

Sure, pick me up at 7?

Absolutely.

I felt guilty. I knew it would make Jordan upset if I went out with Jace, but I didn't care. Neither did Jordan, apparently. I still had received no word from him.

I made my way upstairs and told Russ and Laura what was going down the next night. They seemed supportive, but hesitant.

"I'm not going to lie, I'm rooting for Jordan."

I roll my eyes, "Thanks, Laura."

Russ nods his head agreeing with me. "Remember how he treated you? He was a jerk, for no reason. He's creating, what we call in the tech biz, a pattern."

I know he's right, but I don't want him to be. I want Jordan to be texting me, calling me even, but I sure as heck wasn't going to wait around for him. I'm twenty-three, single, and cute. Why would I wait for a guy that can't bother to text me back?

Not to mention Jordan knows where I live. If it was a problem with the phone, he would know where to find me.

Russ and Laura turn on the TV, while we eat the frozen egg rolls and stir fry. I call it a night at ten. I usually wouldn't be leaving until about thirty minutes from now, but I had a lot on my mind. I say my goodbyes, give my hugs and make my way out the door. Mr. Hidi is standing in the hallway about to enter his apartment.

"You're out and about late," I say with a little concern in my voice. I had never seen Mr. Hidi on my way out, only on the way in.

"My little Georgia isn't feeling too well. I went out to grab some ginger candy to hopefully help."

"Do you need any help?" The words slip out of my mouth, forgetting this was Jordan's grandpa I was talking to.

"No, no, I've got it. Thank you though."

The bags fall from his hands as he fumbles with the key. He's frail and struggles holding many things at once and he knows it.

I pick up the bags while my satchel swings with my body. "After you."

He gives me a big smile and leads me inside. It's just as I envisioned. He has brown leather sofas lining the living room walls, with what I assume is an oak dining table taking most of the room in the kitchen.

"Where do you want these?"

He points to the table that looks well loved.

I set down the bags and start going through them. "What can I hand you first, the ginger ale, or the candy?"

"The M&M's, I'm starving."

I let out a little laugh while I hand him the brown box of plain M&M's. He pops a few in his mouth while I start handing him the other things. I watch him disappear into the bedroom for a few minutes and come back out.

"Thank you, dear, no wonder my Jordan has always thought so highly of you."

I nod not processing what he says. I only fully comprehend the words when I'm back out in the hallway. Highly of me? The kid tortured me for a week straight in eighth grade. Granted, I've been through worse now that I'm older, but that doesn't excuse his behavior. I scoff at the remark. Jordan must have told him about how he offered me a hotel room, but apparently didn't get far enough into the conversation to tell him he has cut me off.

I go back to the elevator where I intended to be originally. Once the elevator shakes on the second floor, I walk out and make my way to 201. I'm shaking, a lot more than I intend to be. I'm crying again. I force myself into my apartment, throw my things on the ground, including my satchel, and go to my bed. These were tears of anger, these were tears of hurt. I don't think I've cried this much since I was a kid.

How could someone offer you a hotel room, buy you lunch, and then cut you off? That didn't seem fair. None of this seemed fair. I took a step back in my mind. Russ was definitely right. It's a pattern, it's a pattern that's been going on forever, and I just hadn't realized it. I wasn't going to let him do this to me. I wipe my tears angrily and put on my pajamas.

When I wake up it's noon. I slept until noon! Crap! Crap! Crap! I am supposed to start my shift right now. Luckily my office is only a few seconds away. I slide on my computer glasses that I rarely wear outside of my home, and make my way to the living room. I pull out my laptop and already have a message from my manager Brody.

"Hey, did you see the file I sent you? It's for some magazine, they think their sales are off, and they are worried about it. Make sure you check it very carefully before sending it back."

I reply with my standard "Sounds good." and clock in. I check my work email and see the file he's talking about. It has over five thousand data points. This is going to take me at least five hours to get through, maybe six if I take a break. I am not going to be late to my date tonight, even if it means asking Brody to log off early.

I'm going through the mess of the data compilations; many of the UPCs and prices don't match up to what their advertisements say. I highlight them all and correct them in a separate sheet. Once I finish, I add the total sales up, and compare them to what the listed prices are supposed to be. They definitely have something to be worried about, they lost out on a few thousand dollars due to the many errors in their system.

I don't know much about computers, but I know how to type and cross reference and that's all you really need to know how to do in this job. That, and as long as you know how to use a calculator, you're all good. I was lucky finding this job a few years back. It was a job not many people wanted to do, so I was paid well. The problem with money isn't that I didn't make enough, it's that I couldn't work during the week like most can. My week was filled with assignments, and taking care of my little brother.

My brother is only sixteen. He is the only sibling I had, and we are eight years apart. My parents worked so much that I spent my days making sure he was fed, and didn't miss the bus. I also help him with homework occasionally, but he's getting to the level of smart that almost surpasses me, so I don't really help that much. This week he was off to a band competition in Washington. Luckily, the bus ride wasn't that long, but almost everyone else in the competition wasn't coming from Idaho, so they had more travel than he did.

Carson comes back on Monday, and I'm supposed to pick him up from his school at four. It's in my calendar, but I'm always worried that I will miss it for some reason. I've never been late when picking him up, or dropping him off on the rare occasion that he missed the bus. I desperately wanted him to get a license, but my parents hadn't had the time to take him, even though he has completed all his driving hours with me. I wish I could take him so desperately, but I know that it has to be his parents or legal guardian, which I am neither of.

I finish off the data, giving it one more look through before sending it off to Brody.

"All done, looks like they had something to be concerned about."

Brody didn't reply, he may have already logged off for the day. He hated confirming clients' worst fears, but if there weren't any concerns with their data it was almost worse, like they paid us to do nothing. I understood, but I was happy I didn't have to deal with them.

I clock out and look at the clock hanging above my T.V. in my living room. 5:52. Perfect, I had just the right amount of time left to get ready. I shut my laptop and stick it back in the red sleeve I used to carry it with me. I occasionally worked from my parents' house, or even Russ and Laura's, but I find having other people around is distracting, so I tend to stick to my own apartment.

I set the sleeve on the coffee table and stand up, stretching every muscle in my body. My bones were always so sore after working from sitting in the same place for hours on end. I make my way to the bathroom and strip my clothes. I cover my hair in a blue shower cap and turn on the water. I'm relieved when it turns on. You go without running water once and it stays with you.

I turn the handle as far left as it goes, making the water hotter than most could handle. I used my time in the showers to unwind from the day, so the hotter the water the more relaxing it was to me. The hot water feels so good on my face, it makes me breathe better, it makes me forget about Jordan, it makes me forget about money, my car and every single worry I have left.

It's six fifteen when I leave the shower. I wrap myself in a towel, and head to my bedroom across the hall. I throw my outfit on the white duvet that encompasses my bed. I decided on a deep green dress. The sleeves flow on my shoulders, and the waist cinches, with the built-in fabric creating a bow at the back. It was my favorite dress; it made me feel really good about myself.

I put the dress on along with my other undergarments and look myself in the mirror. I don't feel super great about what I see. My curls from a few days ago have turned into dark black waves, but my face seems tired and overworked. I feel like this week has been fairly easy, so I'm not sure why. I flatten the edges of my dress and head back to the bathroom to start my makeup. I throw on only the essentials. Concealer, powder, mascara, and I give my eyelashes a little lift with the curler.

"Ow." I pinched my eyelid trying to curl the long lashes attached to it. I hold my hand up to my eye when I hear the knock at the door. It's already seven. I throw on my nude heels, making me about 5'11", and walk towards the door. I pause before answering and throw on some tinted Chapstick from my nude clutch that perfectly matches my shoes. I take a few deep breaths, lower my hand from my eye and open the door.

"Wow." I had no control over that. Every thought and feeling I had about Jordan is gone. Jace stood in front of me with a similar suit to the one Jordan wore the morning of his meetings with the city, except this one looked like it fit Jace like a glove. The only discernible difference in the two suit pieces was Jace wore a nice clean white shirt, while Jordan's was light blue. I push the thoughts of Jordan out of my mind, I was not going to let him ruin this for me. I hadn't been on a proper date since I was twenty and that obviously didn't go as well as we had all hoped.

I didn't date much in high school. I tagged along to many of Russ and Laura's dates, which I'm sure they didn't appreciate. Meeting new people has always been a challenge for me. I think it's partially due to how I grew up, already knowing everyone, and when I didn't know them, I simply stayed clear.

I meet Jace's eyes; they're blue, magnificently blue. I didn't realize that, under the hat he wore while he was working, he had gorgeous light brown hair. The type of brown that could easily be mistaken for dirty blonde it had some redness to it, which is what I saw at the hotel, but definitely wasn't.

"Back at you," Jace said with a half-smile. His hands were in his pockets, and he rocked back and forth on his heels waiting for me to say something.

Jace backs up and gestures a hand down the hallway. "Shall we?"

"Heck yeah we shall!"

Jace laughs fairly loudly, I don't remember it, but I apparently said that out loud. My cheeks get hot. He allows me to step out of the house to meet him outside. I haven't worn heels in a long time so I feel slightly unsteady, but stable enough to walk. The door shuts behind me, and I start walking away.

"You don't think you could go on a date with a locksmith and not lock your door, did you?" He was right. I barely ever forgot to lock my door, but he was making my mind hazy. It felt like I couldn't remember simple things. I run through a list for myself. Phone? Check. Keys? Check. Pepper Spray? Unneeded, but check. Tinted Chapstick? Hopefully I will need to reapply. I turn back towards the door and pull the key from my clutch. It locks with ease, unlike before the key was remade.

"That's some of my finest work right there." Jace points to the key in the lock.

"You did a fantastic job, it works even better than before." I smile back at him. "One question though… you said it would be a day or two, but you got it to me in a few hours. How did you do that?"

He rubs the nape of his neck and looks toward the ground with the half-smile he shared with me before. "Honest?"

"Honest." I reconfirm I want to actually know how he did that so quickly.

"It wasn't finished. I heard Kira telling Jordan she was going to email you to pick up some cord when I got back to Castino's." He takes a deep breath embarrassed, but brings his eyes to mine and lowers his hands back into the pocket of his slacks. "When I heard her talk about how you might be coming, I stopped every other project and got to work. When I went back to the reception desk, you weren't there, so I asked Kira if you bailed and she told me where you were."

"You stopped other projects?"

He nods his head shamefully.

"Thank you." I embrace him for his thoughtfulness and I feel comfortable in his arms as he wraps his hands against my waist.

I let go of him and met his stare. It was one of those stares that you hope something will happen, but I decide not to let something happen. I lean back to tell him to let go of me, without saying something. We stand a foot or two apart just watching each other's faces. It felt like what happens in one of the movies where the main characters finally get together. I hope he's the main character, I would love for him to be the main character.

I grab his hand and we walk towards the elevators, fingers interlocked, swinging with every step. He pushes the down arrow to the left of him and we wait for the doors to open.

"Man, you know about a year ago I wouldn't have had to wait for this elevator. People keep moving in, it's annoying."

He chuckles while I keep my face completely serious. I was serious. I am a very impatient person. We step into the elevator once the doors open. There was an older woman standing in the far right corner.

"Well don't you guys look nice. Going on a hot date?"

We look at each other, fingers still interlocked. I giggle shyly. He nods back at her. Once the elevator reaches the first floor, we start our way into the hallway with the older lady. She turns to make a U-turn. She must be heading to the mail boxes. Jace guides me to his car. It's a black sedan. I don't know enough about cars to know which make and model it is.

He opens my door and I do a little curtsey while I scoot in. While Jace makes his way towards the other side of the car, I study my surroundings. He's got a black ice little tree hanging from his rear-view mirror. It makes his car smell delicious, but also quite fragrant. It almost smells like a middle school locker room where the boys have gotten a hold of too much Axe body spray. Luckily not quite as overwhelming, or I would probably plug my nose the whole ride.

Jace didn't give me much information about where we were going. He just told me to dress nice, which I think I did an OK job at.

"Where are we going?" I ask, dying to know the answer, while Jace backs up the car. He doesn't put his hand on the back of my seat, instead he focuses on the backup camera he has installed. Somehow that broke my heart a little.

"Olive Garden, it's the best place because you can dress up or down and no one will care."

Maybe I'm reading too much into this, but with Jordan I can wear skinny jeans and a sweatshirt and not have one concern. Jace makes me feel as though I have to wear my favorite green dress in order to have a good time.

We made small talk on the way there. I told him a little about my family, but he didn't take very much interest. He explained how fascinating his job is, and how it's so nice that Jordan lets him stay in the hotel as long as he works. I did not want to talk about Jordan. I explain my job, and he nods along which I'm grateful for, because most people cut me off when I start telling them about how interesting data is. People don't realize that my job can very easily make or break a company, just as it did this afternoon with the unnamed magazine shop I went through.

We finally arrived at Olive Garden, and suddenly my spirits were lifted. Olive Garden is good for many things, but my favorite thing is the carbs. Unlimited pasta and bread? Sign me up. He gets out of the car and makes his way to my door. He swiftly opens it and offers me his hand. I take it willingly. Normally after one offers a hand to help someone up, they drop it after, but I didn't. I liked holding his hand. We walk into the noisy restaurant, and on the way through the doors at some point I start holding his bicep with my other hand and lean on his shoulder. He doesn't seem to mind it, so I continue until the waitress shows us to our table.

I walk to pull out the seat opposite of where I assume Jace wants to sit, but he stops me and pulls it out for me. I take a seat and he pushes it slightly in. I blush and look down at the table, while moving some of my hairs out of the way that frame my face. He takes a seat across from me and just smiles. We talk about the menu choices, but I already know what I want. Just like the diner, I found what I liked and stuck to it. He asks me what I plan on getting while interlocking his fingers and setting them sideways on the table.

"Angel hair with Five Cheese Marinara," I say with confidence. I look at him and see him examining my face, smiling. "This is nice." I say to him, hoping he is having the same thoughts, but he simply nods his head and stretches out his right hand.

I place my left hand into his palm. The waitress comes and grabs both our drink and food orders, except I don't get to say a word, Jace orders for me. That makes me smile. We talk about our lives, and Jace explains that he met Jordan years before working at Castino's. Apparently, they went to high school together. I didn't want to be curious about Jordan after we parted ways, but I was. I asked him questions about high school and how they became friends.

"Well Jordan was a very quiet kid, but he was also a trouble maker. We met in detention after he 'accidentally'," Jace makes air quotes with his hands, "forgot to close the door to the reptile cage in biology."

I can't help but laugh, that is totally something Jordan would do. "Well, that doesn't surprise me, but what were you doing in detention with him?

Jace laughs hard enough he leans back and releases my hand. "Well, I may have 'accidentally' taken the lizard out."

I burst out laughing. He seemed to be just as much trouble as Jordan was, but he also seemed to have grown out of it which I need. I needed someone who I could laugh with, but wouldn't make me suffer.

Our food arrives and we both take a minute without talking to eat our food. I'm on my second refill of Diet Coke. Jace doesn't seem to mind; he's on his second glass of Dr. Pepper. Once we're finished with our food, Jace tells me more stories about his high school experience, but I block him out when he mentions Jordan's name. I didn't want to hear about him anymore, just Jace. We decide on no dessert, it's already nine thirty, and we both don't want to stay out too late.

He grabs the check, but only tips 15%. At least he tips, I have to remind myself.

He holds my hand as we walk to the car, but instead of getting in, he leans up against the passenger door, hands holding mine. His thumbs start playing with the back of my hands. This whole situation feels *comfortable*. He pushes himself off of the back door and takes a step closer to me, dropping my hands out of his, and instead replacing them with my soft jawline and waist. I take a few deep breaths and close my eyes, ready for him to kiss me. But it never happens.

I feel Jace's hands drop and I open my eyes with a confused expression on my face. He's looking at something or someone. I follow the directions of his eyes. It's just Jordan. *Jordan. JORDAN.* I see him coming straight at us looking like he's about to kill us both.

Chapter 4

What to do

I looked down on the ground to Jace, his nose bleeding slightly along with his cut lip.

"What was *that*?" I look up with an enormous amount of anger in my voice. My hands are cupped in front of my mouth in awe of what just happened.

Jordan is standing a few feet away from both of us, tending to the fresh cuts that occurred from the amount of force behind that punch. He doesn't look angry anymore, he seems confused almost. His dirty blonde brows furrowing as he looked at what he had done. He rubs his knuckles with his left hand, I don't feel bad about any of it.

"Well, spit it out! What on earth was that for?" Why and how did this man just ruin what should have been a perfect evening. Jace was a lovely gentleman, and now here he was bleeding in the middle of an Olive Garden parking lot.

Jordan starts walking back towards the restaurant as if nothing happened you can see his chest puffing as he walks away. I gave Jace a reassuring look and squeeze to his shoulders that say *I'll be back*. Jace was on the ground now, slumped with his back against the front passenger tire. He seemed just as shocked as I was by what had just happened. I felt bad about leaving him, but I also deserved an answer.

I do my best to catch up to Jordan in the heels I was wearing.

I realized this wasn't going to work. I pause and quickly remove my left, and then right shoe, exposing the newly formed blisters on my feet. I put the heels in my left hand and ran with them dangling against my side. Jordan is close to the doors of Olive Garden by the time I reach him. I put my hand on his shoulder and spun him towards me. He seemed out of breath, like what he did took all of the energy he had. It takes me a few seconds to say anything after looking at him. His entrancing eyes are welled up, the verge of tears ready to be let out. These couldn't be tears of sadness; when someone is sad, they don't punch things, they ball into a corner and cry. If they're like me, they have carbs in the form of sweet desserts. He blinks, letting a single tear fall from his left eye.

I don't know how to act around men when they're upset. Growing up, it was all too common for men to hold in their emotions. That's not the way things were anymore, but I still hadn't gotten used to it. When men were upset in my life, they typically stuffed it in and never showed it to the outside world. It almost made me happy to see a tear on Jordan's cheek; it meant he wasn't hiding anything from me. Instinctively, I put my free hand up to his face and wipe the tear away. We stayed there for a minute, him almost nuzzling and pushing his jaw into the hand that cupped his face. It felt perfect there, almost like that's where it was meant to be. Always.

"Why did you do that, Jordan?"

Me using his name startled him. He pulled his head back and turned around, disappearing into the restaurant. I look through the crowd and watch him push past the hostess stand. He already had a table, or maybe he was just heading to the bathrooms to soothe his raw red eyes and split knuckles. I snap back into reality, remembering who I left behind. I turned away more confused than when I approached Jordan. I slowly made my way back to the car trying to decipher the tears, the face in my palm, everything. Once I'm almost to Jace's car I look down at my hand that once held Jordan's face. Ignoring the urge to run the opposite way and push past the people to find the table or restroom he was located in, I ball my hand in a fist. The nails, freshly manicured, pushed into my skin, creating indents. I reach Jace and take the hand that once held another man and put it up to his face, examining his wounds.

I ask Jace if he's ok.

He replies with a reassuring nod while soothing his jaw. "I've never been punched before. I can now cross that off my list."

I sigh the biggest sigh of relief. If he still has a sense of humor, he's ok. I want him to be ok. I quickly check his pupils, ensuring no signs of a major concussion.

"What list?" Who has a list that includes being punched on it? Do all men have this list? Maybe it was a figure of speech, I never knew when people were being serious or not.

He laughs at me as I help him stand back up. He towers over me, and somehow looks better than before we were interrupted despite his lip and nose.

"I have a list of things I was to experience, but not that I necessarily want to happen…if that makes sense."

I nod along. I do understand. I wouldn't want to be punched either, but there are definitely some things I don't want to go through, but want a taste.

"It's very morbid. I've got things like being bitten by a snake, and a *minor* car crash in there somewhere too." He puts an emphasis on the word minor so I know he doesn't want anyone to be hurt, but maybe just wants the thrill of exchanging insurance information.

I run my thumb over his lips as I assess the damage. Normally I would never be this physical with someone on a first date, but given what just happened I don't think it matters anymore.

"Do you have a first aid kit? You might need some antibiotic ointment on your nose, and you should hold some gauze to your lip for a minute, you may need stitches if it doesn't stop bleeding within the next little while."

He shakes his head no.

"Here, I'll drive to my apartment. I've got a fully stocked one there. You shouldn't be driving after getting hit."

Despite his best efforts, I think Jace knows he shouldn't drive and begrudgingly gets into the passenger seat. I watched him push the chair a little ways back; it was too far up for his long legs to fit. I make my way to the driver's side, still barefoot, and slide into the seat.

I knew that Jace was significantly taller than me, but in the seat, it feels like he's at least a foot or two taller. I start slowly moving the chair towards the steering wheel. The buzz is awkward as the machine does all the work pushing me forward. We sat in silence the entire ride to my apartment. I occasionally glance at his lip, seeing if the bleeding has slowed. It has as we make our way across the city, but he's still having to use his suit jacket to soak blood every once and a while. It needs stitches.

By the time I saw Jordan with a tight fist coming towards us, it was too late. It made me feel unreasonably guilty to think maybe I was at fault for the injuries Jace had just sustained. He had come to punch the crap out of Jace, and I don't know it would have mattered if I had noticed earlier. He was going to do it anyway. He had no right to do that. He had no right to look that *good* doing that. I don't remember it actually happening; I remember the before and the after, but not the actual intense moment. I seemed to do that around Jordan, not remember words, feelings, moments. This time it was out of pure anger though, not attraction. The pattern I try and push the pattern into my mind. Once we arrived at my apartment, I set Jace up on the couch in the living room and disappeared into the bathroom to retrieve my suture kit. He only needed a single stitch on his lip; there was no point in going to the hospital to wait three hours. Before deciding on education, I had taken some basic medical classes. I knew how to do very basic sutures, and I'm not all that great at them, but I can get the job done. Sutures is as far as I got before I realized that I was miserable and didn't want to continue in anything in the medical field. That's why I'm twenty-three still in college for an education degree I definitely should have finished by now.

My heels now by the door giving me free hands, I open the kit that has been under my sink for about two years. I inspect the needle for rust, along with the surgical scissors. I don't see any so I think it's safe to use. I shut it and grab my first aid kit in one hand and suture kit in the other and make my way to the living room.

I set both kits on the table and open the first aid kit.

"Woah, are you accident-prone or something? That is one heck of a first aid kit."

I look up from the contents inside, giving a half smile as I look at Jace. "I went to a few nursing classes fresh out of high school. They gave this to you when you completed the first day of in person training." I start fishing around for the lidocaine cream I know is buried in there somewhere.

"I thought you told me you were in education?" His eyebrows raised.

I try to dull his concerns. "I am, I switched majors when I realized I didn't like people."

He laughs roughly at the fact that I don't like people. "Mm... Ouch." He holds his fingers up to lip. It had cracked slightly more when he laughed. His laugh is the type of laugh I like hearing, but it made me feel nothing like Jordan's laugh did. It wasn't fair comparing the two, but I couldn't get Jordan out of my mind.

After finally finding the lidocaine cream, I put it on the outer edges of his lip and grab a piece of saran wrap and place it on top.

"That should stay on for about fifteen minutes before I start anything." I realize I didn't even ask if I could stitch him up, I was used to doing things without permission. "Are you ok with me doing this?" I didn't notice we were so close to each other until I looked up at his face after asking him.

He gave a sincere smile and nod, wincing at the painful lip.

My green dress spilled over the entire back of me while I worked on his face. I was kneeling in front of him, right in front of his calves. We sat there the entire fifteen minutes, waiting for the timer I had set on my phone to go off. I shiver after my A/C starts blasting throughout the apartment; it feels like I'm up on the fourth floor.

"Here, take this." Jace starts pulling off the sports coat from his shoulders and hands it to me. "I would help you get it on, but..." He points to his hand holding the saran wrap in place.

I smile at the sports coat and gratefully take it from him and slip into it. The sleeves dangle below my wrists so I push them up slightly so I can get to work once the lidocaine numbs the areas near his injury.

The coat is so warm. I've only been offered a coat once, at a high school dance by a random boy that spotted me sticking by

Russel and Laura. He apparently noticed me rubbing my arms. I hadn't been doing that because I was cold, I was just uncomfortable with the crowd. I didn't know how to reject it without hurting his feelings so I took it, trying not to give the impression that I felt so out of place. We didn't end up saying a word the entire night, and I simply returned the coat as we walked out of the college ballroom that was rented out. I never saw him again.

The phone goes off, telling me it's time to wipe the lidocaine off. I disable the timer and carefully take the saran wrap off. He doesn't seem to be in pain with the motion, which means the cream has done an effective job. I give a few test pokes with the tweezers to ensure he is good and numb.

"I suggest closing your eyes. As much of a man as I think you are, it can be frightening watching a needle go through your face."

He does as I say. Honestly if he didn't, I don't think I would have been able to continue. His eyes would have kept me from focusing. I do a simple stitch in his lip and make a knot, then cut the excess with my scissors.

"All done." I smile at my work. I haven't stitched anything in a very long time, so I was impressed.

Jace opens his eyes and smiles right back at me. "Thank you. I didn't feel a thing, you did a great job."

My smile grows at this acknowledgment. It felt good to be recognized for what I did, people don't tell me I do a great job often.

"So… what are the restrictions with having stitches on your mouth? Any activities off limits?"

I start standing up, lightly laughing at what he just said. I know exactly what he was asking, but decided to draw it out anyway. I put all of the supplies away in the bathroom and when I come back, he's standing. He makes long strides towards me that make me freeze.

"You didn't answer my question." His hand is now caressing my face and I start breathing a little quicker. He leans in, this time I interrupt.

"Unfortunately, no activities until that comes out." I point to the thread attached to his lips.

His head falls back and his hands drop. "Well then I should go, I might break that rule if I stick around any longer." He rolls his eyes as he says it.

I laugh again. Jace makes me laugh a lot. It's nice having him around. Even though we just met a few days ago, I already look forward to seeing him again. I hope that he wants to see me again.

We start making our way to the door. I open it for him, and he starts walking out.

He half turns once he meets the door frame. "I had a nice time."

I lean against the door I'm holding. "Me too." I smile as I say it, but it's not a grin by any means. I take my head off of the dark brown door and my smile fades. "I'm sorry about tonight, I don't know what he was doing… I don't know why…"

He interrupts me, scratching the base of his neck with his right hand. "I do. He likes you. I asked him before I asked you out and he said there wasn't a problem, but obviously that's not the case." His words took mine. It takes me a second before I can speak.

I looked towards the floor at the door frame. "That's not true. If he liked me, he wouldn't go around punching the people I want to hang out with."

"You want to hang out with me?" His voice echoes through my head.

"I do. I know tonight was awful towards the end, but I enjoyed it up until that point."

"Me too, I would love to go out again. That is, if I have the money. I don't know if I have a job right now." Nervous laughter escapes him. I forgot he worked for Jordan.

I respond just as nervous as his laugh. "You should sue for employer harassment or something." We meet eyes again.

"I will. Goodnight Anna."

"Goodnight." I shut the door as he turns and makes his way towards the elevator.

I didn't really get a chance to really process what happened back at the restaurant. Once the door is closed, I sag downwards against the door and start sobbing. I'm hit with a wave of emotion I wasn't expecting. I don't know why I'm crying. I wasn't the one punched in the face. I didn't tell Jordan to do that.

After quite a while, I get myself off the floor and make my way to my room to change. I realize I'm still wearing Jace's sports coat. I hang the coat on the back of my door and slip my dress off and put it back in my closet, separate from my other clothes, as a note to myself that I need to take it to the dry cleaners. I slip on one of my infamous Hard Rock sweatshirts, this one is from New York. I put on my bright blue workout pants that have never actually been worked out in, but they make for a good pant alternative. Once changed, I go to the bathroom and take off my makeup, wash my face and brush my teeth.

After the night I've had I'm exhausted. I suspect I'll fall asleep very quickly. I lay down in bed, turn off my lamp, and close my eyes. The opposite of what I expected happens. I'm wide awake. I can't stop thinking about what Jace said about

Jordan. After about thirty minutes of this I turn my lap back on and sit up with my back against the headboard. I bring my knees to my chest and stare at the wall opposite of my bed.

How would Jace know how Jordan felt about me? Did they discuss it? Or was it based on a suspicion? Jordan barely knew me; I've changed a lot since eighth grade. He couldn't feel what Jace stated he felt, it didn't make sense. Then again, it didn't make sense how he had treated me the past few days. I shook the thoughts out of my mind. The way I was thinking was insane. I just watched Jordan punch a guy. Not only did he punch someone, he punched the only person I'm attracted to. *Stop.* No more thoughts about Jordan. Not cool me. I lay down on my side and turn off my lamp. After laying for about an hour in the dark I finally fell asleep.

Sunday night comes and goes in a blur. Work, break, work, repeat. Jace hasn't texted me yet. It makes my heart sore, and leaves a heavy feeling in my chest. Jordan hadn't changed. I don't know why I expected him to be such a different person then who he was ten years ago. I had changed, but that doesn't mean he had.

Once the day of work ends, I check my phone again. I tell myself I can't text Jace, I don't want to pressure him into another date. I wouldn't want to go on a second date either if I were him. My thumb hangs over the J section of my touchscreen. Jordan is there. I click on the contact information and stare. I don't even have his cell phone, only the phone sitting in his office at Castino's. I go to exit and put my phone face down on the couch that I had started to leave indentations for sitting in for such long periods of time.

Hello? Hello? Annie? I look down at my phone sitting on the couch. I know what happened but don't want to believe it.

After gaining enough courage, I turn my phone over and stare at the phone call in progress. Despite every bone in my body telling me to put it up to my ear, to hear his voice, to hear the voice I crave and want, I hover once more above the phone screen, my thumb begging to end the call, but every other part of me wants to stay on.

I slowly lift the phone up to my ear but don't mutter a sound. "Annie? I know you're there, I can hear you breathing on the other line." I hold my breath reflexively. I must sound like one of the serial killers you see in movies who just breathe into the phones until they pop out of nowhere to kill you.

"Annie…I'm so…" He sighs deeply, I can hear the regret in his voice, but what he did was inexcusable. "I'm so sorry. Jace and you didn't deserve that. You two looked like you were having a good time and I was there for a business dinner, and I saw you and… and I just… well I don't know." He trails off into silence.

We both sit there breathing into the phones for at least five minutes. It sounds like he's interrupted by a knock on his door, but I can't make out the sounds on his end very clearly. "You don't have to listen to me now, but every day I'll try and make it up to you, so you know how much I'm sorry. I'll be in my lobby every day at two. If you decide to show up at some point, I'll take you to the diner and we can talk. Until then I'm so, so sorry Annie."

The line disconnects, but my ear is still held up to my speaker for what feels like an inexplicable amount of time.

Finally, the phone drops from my hand. My right palm is still facing my ear as if nothing has changed and I'm still on a call. Tears flood my eyes and fall to my red warm cheeks. It was a silent cry, an 'I don't know what I'm doing' cry. The type of cry that takes every ounce of energy from you despite how quiet it is cry. Why was I letting this man, who I barely have a friendship with, get to me so much? Why was I letting someone I previously hated, and never wanted to see again, give me *butterflies*? My stomach tangles when I hear him, when I see him, when I think of him. I realize the cry I'm having is a pitiful cry, I pitied myself so deeply. I let someone entangle themselves in me, and I didn't even see it coming. I didn't stop it. A mess was made because of seeing him, and there was no way I could clean it up.

Chapter 5

Waiting

A week went by without any interaction with the outside world. I wasn't living in my body. I felt like I was on autopilot. I ran my errands, I went to Laura's and Russell's apartment, picked up my brother from camp, and that was it. I pretended nothing had happened, but somehow pretending nothing had happened affected my life. When I went to run errands, I went a few towns over to their grocery store. It took me twenty-three minutes there and back, but it was worth it. The thoughts of running into Jordan in the grocery store haunted me, and I hadn't been back to Josie's since. I avoid Castino's unless I absolutely have to pass it, and every time I do I look for his car, along with Jace's. I feel so bad for Jace. All he did was go to Olive Garden and now he's checking off his list.

My brother got first place in his competition. I remember taking him out to dinner with my parents, but that's all I remember about what he told me about how Washington was. My father belittled me about dropping out of a 'worthy' profession, and my mother worried about how I would pay my bills. This happened all the time. I still remember my father's face when I told him I was switching to a teaching major, I swear I almost killed him. He tried for weeks to convince me to do anything but teaching. Accounting. Sales. Law school. Anything. I was spoken to by different members from those respecting departments about what they do, despite my stance. It took me a while to accept that I just wasn't cut out for a job like that. I wanted to be creative and helpful, but most of all I wanted to know I was doing something every day to put a smile on someone's face. Everything else around me seems to go in fast forward, and slow motion all at the same time.

Monday at one thirty. That meant, in approximately thirty minutes, Jordan would be standing in the lobby of Castino's waiting for me and being disappointed every time. Something happened today though. I grabbed all of my things and slammed my door behind me as I exited my apartment complex. I had built up some steam that was ready to be released. I run down the stairs and get to my car. I slide into the driver's side and slam the door with enough power that it sticks on the first try. My key goes into the ignition, and before I know it, I'm halfway to the hotel. I had left Jordan waiting every single day at two P.M. and it wasn't my intention to not leave him waiting, but I was just angry enough to know that if I didn't say something now, I never would.

1.52. I'm in the parking lot sitting, waiting. My nerves start to make a reappearance and I drive around the block a few times to soothe them. Once I'm back I don't even look at my clock. I know it's around two and I needed to go in now, before my legs decided they simply couldn't move.

I storm through the automatic doors and my eyes immediately dart to Kira. She's happy to see me, but she can tell I am not happy to be here.

"Where is he?" I've never heard my voice so angry, but it wreaths with exasperation.

She points towards his office, a little bit scared. I stomp over and set my things forcefully down on the reception desk as I get there. I was definitely making a scene, but I didn't care. I keep walking down the hall and make a sharp turn when I run into him. He was on his way to the lobby.

I stare at him with so much fire in my eyes and I think he knows I'm not there to forgive and forget, but much rather give him a stern talking to. I back away from him quickly and meet his eyes. He shamefully hangs his head, knowing what he did was wrong. He can't meet my eyeline without just as quickly staring down at the floor once again.

"How could you?" My hands are flailing everywhere. "How could you do that to me? You don't even know me. Two days don't make up for how you treated me when we were kids. You were ruthless. I was called "Stinkerbell" for weeks following that dance, and it didn't stop there. Kids didn't stop calling me that until after high school. I was happy with Jace, and you ruined it like you ruin everything." I didn't understand that so much of my anger was due to how he treated me as a kid.

He finally meets my face. His eyes filled with confusion, as if what I said didn't make any sense to him.

"Are you going to punch out any guy who tries to kiss me? Do I need to leave?" Still making eye contact, my tone has shifted. I'm no longer shouting, but the anger and hurt is still there.

He grabs my left hand, but I pull back immediately. I was not going to get flustered and ruin the speech I had prepared. He grabs it once more, this time holding on tight enough that I wasn't *couldn't* physically go anywhere. I had tears streaming heavily on my face.

"Please don't leave." His voice was soft and smooth, like me threatening to move out of this forsaken town was the same as putting a knife through his heart.

"Once a douche canoe, always a douche canoe." I poked my

right hand fingers into his chest as I said that. My voice was serious, but a little lighter than my original yelling.

He grabs my right hand, but keeps it where my fingers were touching. He leans into my ear, and suddenly the only sensation I have is his breath against my face. "Did you just call me a douche canoe?" He makes a slight laugh into my ear as he whispers his ridiculous question. Still holding onto my hands, he moves his face back into my line of sight. That smirk that I hate so much on his lips.

"Of course I called you a douche canoe. That's what you are? You're a big douche canoe who can't figure out how to not ruin things." I'm trying my best not to laugh, but instead keep a serious tone.

"What even is a douche canoe?" He starts looking puzzled.

"Well, if you look up douche canoe in the dictionary you will find a giant picture of your—"

I'm cut off by his hands now clenching my face. His lips are on mine. My body tenses at the touch at first, but despite every want and every need I have, I sink in. He kisses like he's been holding it in for years and finally let go, even though the desire is new He wasn't waiting anymore. My lips still pushed outward and eyes still closed. I feel his hands drop to my wrists, which had somehow found their way by themselves to the middle of his back. He backs away until he has the palm of his hands surrounding mine. I open my eyes blinking a few times, as if I need to force myself to think clearly.

"Jordan—I…"

He's smiling again. He knows what he just did to me. He knows he gave me butterflies.

Chapter 6

405

Before I know it, I'm halfway through the hotel. I grab my stuff in one swift motion, still sitting on the reception desk. As I walk, almost running to the doors, I place two fingers from my right hand on my bottom lip. He just kissed me and my brain can't comprehend how I went from yelling to yearning. It takes everything in me to try not to look back, but I did anyway. Jordan is standing at the end of the hallway close to his office, watching me leave. He looks disheveled. He's running his hands through his hair and puffing his cheeks out like he doesn't know what just happened, like he didn't just do that to me.

Jordan's reaction tells me this wasn't planned. It was spontaneous and not meant to have happened. It doesn't change that it did. I make it to my car, but this time I don't have the energy to shut my door. I sit in the upholstered seat sideways and push both of my hands to my face. I feel like crying, but nothing comes out. Pushing my hands through my hair, I take a deep breath while I readjust into my seat. It takes me a minute to start the car and finally shut the door over and over, each with a growing frustration at the situation. I half expect Jordan to bust through the front of the doors and find me, but he doesn't. I get them again once I'm situated. The butterflies. My stomach twists and turns and almost makes me want to throw up in the best way possible. I get them often when I'm around Jordan. That kiss made them run wild, which I hadn't felt before.

"Listen here butterflies, y'all need to find somewhere else to go, ok?" I'm poking and prodding at my stomach hoping the imaginary butterflies will go away, it didn't seem to be working as I had hoped. Once my stomach has settled down, and my cheeks begin to even out, I start driving.

I'm at my apartment complex in the blink of an eye. I've been trying to use the stairs more often, but I make my way to the elevator through the lobby after I gather my things I feel dizzy while walking. I touch my lips again. For some reason I want to wash them; maybe it's a sensory thing, or maybe it's because if I did end up kissing Jordan Myers, I didn't want it to be like that. I want a do over, I demand one. I finally get to the arrow and press the up button. It's only two thirty, but I hope Laura is home from work. She sometimes gets off a little early on Mondays, depending on how busy her office is.

Mr. Hidi is in the elevator with me. I made the doors reopen shortly after he had stepped in. I feel all the blood rush to my face.

"You look like you've had an afternoon." His hands are overlapped sitting in front of him. While he speaks, he turns and half smiles at me. Apparently smirks run in the family.

"I have, but I think I'm ok now."

"I hope so. You know he didn't mean to hurt you. I haven't seen my grandson so happy since meeting you."

My eyes widen to the point it felt like they were about to fall out. I remember who I'm talking to. Mr. Hidi is Jordan's grandfather.

The word grandfather tastes weird in my mouth. I grew up only knowing one side of my family, or at least visiting only one side of my family. We were so casual growing up. We didn't dress up to see each other on holidays, or go to my grandparents' home bearing gifts. Sometimes we would even just stop by unannounced to sit on their couch and watch the cooking channel. They were my comfort as a kid. It was hard for me to imagine anything different.

I was always pressured to do well by my parents as a kid. When I was a kid, it was hard having parents constantly remind you that you weren't doing enough. It grew into this awful pressure that I was a failure up into high school. I was lucky to have Russ and Laura in high school, otherwise I wouldn't have made it. I was doing every extra-curricular you could imagine, every AP class, every fair, and I worked a part time job. I stretched myself so thin that I cried almost every day over test scores, or not being able to accomplish what I wanted. Many times, I would find Russ or Laura and just sob into them. They tried so many times to get me to drop some of the weight on my shoulders, but I felt like I couldn't. I didn't want to disappoint my family. It made me even more reliant on my grandparents due to this.

Once I graduated high school, I took a gap semester. I graduated with Honors, and was beat out for valedictorian, which I felt was a huge disappointment, but my parents didn't seem to mind. My dad was the only one working when I was in school, which made the pressure even heavier because I had one parent to always remind me of what I couldn't accomplish. My gap semester was filled with absolute nothingness. I didn't work, I didn't go to school, I didn't do anything. It was, and still is the only time in my life I had done nothing. The first month or two was extremely hard for me. The feeling of pressure to work and go to school consistently weighed on me, but that was when my mom decided to return to work and when I helped out around the house with my little brother.

I was never asked to help with my brother, but it was a way for me to do *something* without doing too much. After I went back to school and found the job I still currently have, I continued helping, because I don't know how to stop. I don't really know if I'll ever stop. It makes me feel like I can do something that I know is helpful, even if my parents don't.

Throughout the semester I took off from life, my parents and I would fight, not just bicker, but yell and scream at each other. We would fight what seemed like all of the time. They wanted me to get a job, and when I would, I didn't make enough for them. They wanted me to start school, which I completely ignored; I was still trying to figure out what I wanted to do, and I didn't want to waste any time. During these fights, I would long for my grandparents, but somewhere down the line we stopped randomly dropping in, and I knew it wasn't ok to simply stop by anymore. It warmed my heart that Jordan took care of his grandparents, like I wish I would with mine.

When I was a kid, it was so different. If my parents and I were fighting, my grandma would come in her gray minivan and pick me up for a sleepover. It helped both my parents and I to cool down. We spent the night watching movies, eating McDonalds, and in the morning, she would make me white bread toast cut in those little triangles with a slab of crunchy peanut butter on top. Those mornings were something I looked forward to often. We were the family who only ever had wheat bread in our home for the majority of my life. Tasting sweet bread was a rare treat, and even now it reminds me of those mornings where everything was ok, even if it was just for a minute. Once I was back home the morning after a fight, it was never spoken about. My parents didn't do well with their feelings. It was simply ignored and we would go about our day. I think that is what makes me try to avoid their house as an adult: I now hate fighting that can't be resolved. I think ultimately that's why I decided to go confront Jordan.

I return a half smile to Mr. Hidi. "Thanks, I know he didn't mean to hurt me, but he did. I just don't think that I can handle that right now." I place my hands in a similar fashion to him, curling my lips inward in hopes that he would see that the conversation was making me uncomfortable.

He takes a deep breath in. "You're going to have to eventually talk to him, especially if you go to that reunion at the end of August."

"What reunion?" I turn to face him with a raised eyebrow of concern. I do not have it in me to see anyone from my past.

"Your old charter school is being reformed as a public middle school, so they're having a reunion for all of the eighth grade classes that graduated there. You didn't see the letter?"

I make a small gasping sound. I realize that I haven't checked my mail in the past week since I've been in an emotional slump. "No, I haven't, but I'll go check the mail once I check in with Laura."

He gives a slight nod and turns back as the doors open, gesturing for me to exit first.

"Thank you, Mr. Hidi, you're always so wise." I give him a smile as I follow his gesture through the opened doors.

He says nothing, and simply makes his way to his apartment. I stop a door before him and knock on the door. I close my eyes tightly and hope to myself that Laura is inside somewhere.

"Woah, are you OK?" Laura swings the door open very casually. Apparently the way my face hung already said how I was feeling.

I can't speak, I only look towards the old carpet and shake my head no. This time the tears start flowing down my red hot cheeks. Tears have been coming down my face a lot more than usual since Jordan has come around. He still holds the same amount of power that he did in eighth grade, maybe even more. I never got those stupid butterflies until seeing him as an adult and I wasn't going to let flying bugs determine my feelings.

Laura escorts me to the couch with one hand on my back. I shiver at the touch; it felt like only one hand belonged there, and it wasn't meant to be Laura's. She seems to notice and removes herself completely from my spine. Once to the couch, she touches my arms and sits on the edge of the worn-down wood coffee table.

"Did someone hurt you?" She is still touching the sides of my arms in attempts to comfort me.

I don't know how to answer that. How can I explain that someone hurt me by being the most handsome and caring person I know?

"No, he didn't hurt me." I have to break in between my words for sniffling and tear wiping.

After taking a sigh of relief, Laura stands up and walks to the kitchen. She fills an electric kettle and starts the water on the 'green' setting. Not a single word is spoken during this time.

Once the kettle has heated up to temperature, she brings in two cups and sits on the chair on the other side of the table. She slides me a cup, a tea bag dangling out of it, and slowly starts sipping on her own, careful not to burn herself.

Something comes over me, and I just let everything out. The date with Jace, the punch, the stitches, and *the kiss*. I was so lucky to have met Laura. She was the best listener I had ever met. She knows how to sit and knows when not to say anything. It made me even more happy that Russ kept her around which meant I also got to keep her. Once I'm done talking and my tears have dried, Laura stands up. She picks up the mugs, mine still half full, and makes her way to the kitchen and gently sets them in the sink. Once she comes back, she stands in front of me, and it forces my eyes upward to meet her face. The long arms attached to her body are outstretched. Until now I didn't realize what I really needed, which was a hug.

She embraces me in a way that makes me immediately calmer. I hug her back with my face in her deep brown hair, and we just stand there, hugging for what seems like an hour or two. Eventually she lets go and grabs onto my shoulders to look at me again.

"I'm sorry you like him, I'm sorry that he kissed you, I'm sorry."

For some reason, that soothes me even more, I feel awful admitting this, but I don't want to like Jordan, I don't want him kissing me. I'm sorry too. I'm sorry for the butterflies that will have to go away, I'm sorry for the way I lead Jordan on, I'm sorry for so many things.

After sitting on the couch for at least two hours while Laura does house chores, I get up and let her know I need to go get my mail.

"Just walk right in when you're back, I'll keep the door unlocked."

I wasn't intending to come back, but maybe I needed to.

I took the elevator back downstairs. Complete silence overwhelmed me. I felt slightly better after talking (more like complaining, rambling) to Laura.

When I reach my mailbox, it is labeled with the number corresponding to my apartment. I pull the keychain out of my satchel and stare down at the keys hanging off of them, the gold key that Jace made me still shiny and new, reflecting off of something. It created a light orb that danced around the room. I played with the light, making it do whatever I wanted. The control felt so good after the past few weeks I had. After I finished, I opened the mailbox. Mostly junk mail was in there, a few newspapers, a pamphlet from Castino's which I'm sure was placed in everyone's mailbox, but felt like a personal attack. I immediately went to the communal trash can and threw it away with force. Once I returned from throwing that away, I continued getting my week-old mail. There was the envelope that Mr. Hidi talked about.

It was a deep navy envelope with gold trimming and a rose wax seal also in gold, keeping the letter sealed. The paper of the envelope felt so smooth on my hands; the envelope felt like it fit right into my palm. My original plan was to throw the envelope away as soon as I laid my eyes on it, but instead I shoved the letter into my bag and locked up my mail slot. I double checked for packages, which I rarely ever had since I couldn't really afford to shop online.

A package sat in the slot P1 for me. I racked my brain for what I could've ordered, and nothing came to mind. Whatever it was, it was wrapped in a white bubble mailer, so it must be fragile. There isn't much information on the packing sticker other than some distributor's name and my name, along with the address of my apartment. "What are you?" I inspect and flip the package, hoping it'll answer me.

I closed the package slot and made my way up to Laura and Russ's apartment, still trying to determine what was in the package, or if it was some practical joke.

Once reaching the fourth floor, I walk into their apartment

without knocking. Russ was now home, even though it wasn't quite yet five o'clock.

"So, Laura filled me in on some pretty wild things, are you OK?"

Am I OK? What type of question is that? I give him a blank stare with a few sassy slow blinks in between in hopes he would figure it out by himself.

"I'm going to guess that, based on the rate of your eyelids, you are in fact not OK." I nod in agreement.

"That would be a correct assumption." My voice seems a little lower than normal, like I had just woken up, but ultimately, I think it was due to the amount of crying over the past little while. Sometimes I would cry without even realizing it, and I would only notice when I would look down and see little wet spots over my pants.

Russ removes himself from the kitchen where he was just starting dinner. Fettuccine alfredo is what it looks like he was making. Once he reaches my sad limp body in front of the door, he hugs me tighter than ever before. Russ always gave the best hugs. They were the type of hugs you wanted every day, the type that girlfriends should get jealous of, and in this moment, I was immensely grateful that Laura let me hug Russ like this. She knew I needed it; she always knew what I needed.

"So, what's that?" Russ releases the hug with a raised eyebrow and points at the package I have in my hand. He tried to snag it from me, but I was too quick when putting it behind my back.

"I have no clue, and I am sure as heck I'm not going to let you find out before me." I race over to the couch, Russ following me like a lost puppy, when Laura comes and joins us.

We all stare at the package with great intensity when Laura

finally speaks. "Well open it! I'm dying over here." She starts reaching and grabbing for it.

I look at the white bubble mailer one last time before ripping the seam that states 'tear here'. I hand the tab of the bubble mailer to Russ, who keeps it in his hand instead of throwing it away.

My nerves were getting to me. Did someone die, and this is their last testament? No, that can't be it, no one would trust me to handle their belongings. Was it some prank, and I was going to find myself staring into a potato-gram? I hope so, because there are a lot of worse alternatives running through my mind right now.

I finally gained the courage to look inside after taking a few deep breaths. With one more large breath I extracted the white fabric that was inside and unfolded it. It was a Donny Osmond t-shirt, the exact same one I wore in the grocery store that day. I couldn't believe he was able to find it, let alone in my size. These shirts typically are sold only on tours and then never seen again. A giggle escapes my lips.

My face lights up when I realize what it was, and I have to manually swipe the large grin off of my face. "He did it, that douche canoe did it," I whisper to myself happily.

Russ goes and throws the white tab away I handed him earlier.

"There's something else in there." Laura grabs the package that was still sitting on my lap and pulls out a cling wrapped black square. "Oh my gosh. Anna, look?"

I finally pull my face away from the shirt in front of me and look at what she was trying to show me. She turns it around from her, so that I can see the front.

"Holy crap!... Sorry." I realized I yelled that instead of using my inside voice.

It was a signed vinyl of my favorite Donny Osmond album: 'From Donny…with love.' I stare at the bottom left-hand corner, where the gold sharpie had a customized message: 'Annie, thank you for all of the support throughout the years. I hope you enjoy. Signed Donny Osmond.'

"Woah, that man really wants you to forgive him," Russ chimes in, stirring the alfredo portion of the fettuccine alfredo he's making.

"Yeah, but he had to have sent this earlier than today. I mean, it wouldn't be here the same day he bought it."

"Do you not remember him punching your date in the face? I would say that's probably when he bought his apology gift." Russ seems almost upset in his voice, like I shouldn't be accepting, let alone be so enthused by these gifts. He points the sauce covered spoon at me from the kitchen.

I look up at him from the shiny vinyl sitting in my hands. He definitely isn't happy, but I don't know that I could blame him. I'm not excited to be receiving gifts from someone who is literally awful to everyone around me.

Changing the subject, I pull out the envelope from my bag, setting aside the gifts I just received. "Are you going to this?" I wave the envelope in my hand catching his attention.

He turns his back to me and continues stirring his sauce.

Laura interjects, placing her hand on my shoulder to reassure me. Hopefully, Russ is just in a mood. "We can't go, Russ was asked to go to California the same week to meet with some software developer, and he wants me to go with him."

Laura removes her hand from my shoulder, and I look back at Russ. "Congratulations, that must mean you're doing something right." I give him a very sarcastic thumbs up.

He barely looks over his shoulder. That's it, I've had it. I don't deserve to be treated this way, especially over a boy.

"What is wrong with you? Did I do something? Why are you acting like this?" I'm yelling again, but this time I feel no need to apologize. Russ is a very direct person, based on how he's been dancing around the current topic, I knew he didn't have the best opinion.

Russ turned around, a little shocked, but it also looked like he was expecting me to finally burst. Laura puts her head in between her knees in silence. She knows what's going on, they're keeping something from me, and we've never kept anything to ourselves.

"Laura?" I'm now standing and looking down at her.

She just shakes her head.

"Wow… OK, you know what? If you guys don't want to tell me, that's fine, but I'm not sticking around for this." I start gathering my things quickly, and double check to make sure I have all of my belongings.

As I start walking towards the door a knock halts my progression. It doesn't sound like it's coming from outside this apartment, but it was forceful.

"Wallace Fire, we got a call?" Someone is shouting from outside of the door.

We all pause and look at each other, not really knowing how to proceed. I put my things down and race to the door. Russ and Laura follow. I open the door with more force than I intend. Georgia is laying on the stretcher, oxygen hooked up into her nose. Mr. Hidi is slowly following behind, trying to catch up with the EMTs. He's still wiping tears from his face, letting out silent sobs.

"Oh my gosh, what happened?" The words escape my mouth before I even get the chance to think.

"She collapsed. My sweet Georgia collapsed," Mr. Hidi replies, wiping tears in his eyes while his wide framed glasses began to fog up.

Before I knew it, I was offering to drive him to the hospital to meet paramedics there. The EMTs offered to take him in the ambulance, but he told them he didn't think he could handle seeing her if something happened on the way. I don't know how he thought so logically in such a scary moment.

We all squished into my old hunk of junk car and started our way to Providence Hospital. Everyone, including Russ and Laura. Now was not the time to figure out the weird vibe that happened earlier. Our focus was on Georgia and Georgia alone.

Georgia Hidi was one of the sweetest humans I had ever met in my entire life. Before she got too old and frail, she was that neighbor who would bake cookies and bring them over while they were still steaming, just because she wanted to see you take the first bite. Russ and Laura eventually had to tell her to stop bringing food over after both of them gained twenty pounds each. She didn't really stop though, they just became more infrequent, or she would try out a new recipe for 'healthy' cookies that used applesauce as a substitute, or bananas or whatever the recipe called for.

About six months ago, she got an infection in her lungs and hasn't been the same since. Every single person on the fourth floor, along with me, would check on her. Eventually, Mr. Hidi couldn't take the stress of hosting visitors while taking care of her, full time.

The last time I saw her was when I offered to help Mr. Hidi with his groceries. I saw her through the doorway that led to the master bedroom in their two-bedroom apartment. She was sleeping, almost a little too deep for the time that it was. She had this puffy permed white hair that had fallen flat in a few places. I assumed she hadn't gotten it done since being sick. It was fairly short, and almost resembled the volume and hairstyles of the late 80s.

She typically wore glasses, very similar to her husbands, but I remember seeing them sitting on the nightstand I could barely make out in the line of vision I had. Seeing her like that made me realize why Mr. Hidi hadn't had visitors; she required round the clock care, and trying to give that to her while trying to talk to someone just wasn't possible. The last conversation I had with Georgia was a night she brought me cookies. She usually just brought over two plates to Laura and Russ's house, but eventually when she got to know me, she started bringing them down directly to me. It was one of the sweetest things I could have imagined. I was worried when I first moved out that I wouldn't be friends with anyone other than Russ and Laura.

She had a thick southern accent, and when asked about it, she would always make the same joke. "Guess where I'm from?"

She always waited for people to take the most obvious guess.

"Wrong, Louisiana." She always got a kick out of correcting people. Just because her name was Georgia didn't mean that is where she was from, and to her it was hilarious.

Mr. Hidi had a similar issue. He was adopted by two Indian parents in secret when he was born. He went by Hank Jefferson for most of his life, to try not to upset people that his parents weren't the same color as him. Once it became acceptable, he finally started using his real name. According to him, seeing a white child with brown parents when he was young was preposterous. Before he realized what he needed to do, there were many times that he pretended he had no clue who his parents were. The first time I heard that story my heart broke. Imagine having to fake who your parents are to the world, just because of their skin.

I started parking the car, my stomach now sour and cramping with emotion as I thought back to the times I had with the Hidis. Georgia was one of those people you just never thought would get to this point, and I didn't know that I could take going in there. If I didn't know what Anik (that was Mr.Hidi's first name) was going through, I honestly probably wouldn't have gone inside.

Once the car was fully in park, Mr. Hidi grabbed my hand over the console. He needed to take a few breaths before he walked into whatever he was about to walk into. I just looked at him while we both shed a tear together and waited for his signal.

Eventually, we all got out of the car and made our way to the waiting room. Anik talked to a few people to try and figure out what happened, but everyone had the same response.

"We're still running a few tests, we will let you know when we have the results."

I was angry for him. That was his wife, and no one would even give him the decency to tell him something, anything! Russ and Laura both had to calm me down a few times.

I, on many occasions, started walking towards the reception desk, before I was reminded each time: "If they aren't telling the spouse anything yet, what makes you think they're going to tell the neighbors."

They were both right, no one was going to tell me anything, but that didn't change how upset I was.

I watched the automatic doors swing open at the emergency room entrance multiple times over ten, maybe fifteen minutes. It was agony knowing that not a single soul was going to come through those doors that could help make anything go any faster.

I had to force myself to stop watching the doors; it was

making my mind go numb. We all had taken a seat and moved around a few times, scattering in the waiting area. Sitting was no longer an option for me, I couldn't sit still anymore.

Leaning against a wall seemed to be working for me. I crossed my arms across my chest so I wouldn't keep picking at my skin. It was an anxious habit. Despite forcing myself not to, when I hear the sounds of the automatic doors, I look up.

Jordan is standing in the middle of the waiting area now, and he makes his way to the reception desk to try and find out where his grandmother…grandma is.

"Jordan, over here." I wave him over, and he smiles at the receptionist to let her know he's found his group of people. It'es weird that I'm a part of his group of people.

He's walking a little quicker than normal over to me and embraces me in one of the tightest hugs ever. I have to remember this isn't a hug because he likes me, it's a solemn hug, the hug to give someone who's grieving, and that's all I could do right now, was be the person he hugged. I tried not to let my feelings get in the way of letting him have his own.

At this point, we were just waiting for anything. An ounce of information at this point would be better than nothing, but we aren't getting anything. Jordan and I were leaning up against the wall next to each other, biceps touching. He was wearing a suit, but the tie was loosened and the top two buttons undone. I assume he was at some sort of meeting when he got the call.

Laura and Russ were in chairs at the other end of the waiting room, consoling each other, while Mr. Hidi walked around, talking to doctors and disappearing for short periods of time to what I assume is go to the room she was in, finding any piece of information he possibly can.

"I know this may not be the best time, but I got your

package." I look up at Jordan, who hasn't moved his eyes from the floor until now, when he meets mine. It feels so natural looking at him like this, like he's the only person in the entire room.

He doesn't say anything for a minute, he just grins. "Did I do OK? I wasn't sure if it was the exact same one, or if I got the wrong one…" He sounds worried, even though he shouldn't be.

I unwrap one of my arms and grab his bicep. "You did amazing." My voice is calm, hopefully reassuring in such an unsure moment.

He unfolds both of his arms and hugs me again. This time it isn't one of those tight hugs, it was a hug like what Russ usually gives, except somehow better. This was a caring hug.

"I am so, so sorry. You didn't deserve your date to be ruined and I can't believe I kissed you like that. You were right, I am a douche canoe." He's whispering his warm breath into my scalp. I knew he was tall, but this hug made me realize just how tall is. One hand travels up my back and is pushing my face into his chest, while the other rests in its original position. I don't say anything back. I think he just needs to be for a moment.

Wetness begins to intrude my hair; he's crying. They are the same sobs I've been having for the past week, silent, but necessary. I hug him tighter than I did before, and he releases me as soon as I do. He wipes his cheeks while he looks at me, eyes now burning with redness from the salty tears that he just dropped.

Our arms are still holding onto each other, but now the rest of our bodies are at least six inches apart. We just watch each other, except unlike the previous times we've held each other's gaze, I don't think either of us plan to look away.

What he says next is not what I expected to come out of his

mouth. "You and Jace would be good together. You should give it a shot."

My hands drop to my sides, but he remains in place. I force them off of my body by turning so my back is against the wall again. "Thanks, but he hasn't texted me since you almost punched his lights out." My arms are folded again, hopefully this time they behave.

"... That may be my fault." His voice lowers in volume, and he starts raking his fingers through his hair.

"What?... What do you mean that is your fault?" I turned to him, eyebrows raised. Did this man just admit to me that he blocked me from possible forever happiness? How freakin' rude.

"I told him he could keep his job if he didn't go out with you again." Jordan is staring at the floor again, hopefully ashamed. What kind of person does this?

Without any hesitation, I pull out my phone and call Jace. It rings a few times before I finally reach him.

"Hey, Anna. Look, I'm sorry I haven't called it's… it's just complicated." His voice is straining, like he hopes nobody can hear him.

"It's not complicated, apparently you have a boss who thinks it's OK to interfere with your personal life. Jordan told me what he did. That's actually why I'm calling, I would love to go out again. This time hopefully you don't need any stitches." I laugh a little into the phone and watch Jordan become uncomfortable. Good, I hope he's uncomfortable. He deserves to never be comfortable again after what he pulled.

"Are you sure? I mean, I won't get in trouble at work?"

I shake my head even though Jace can't see me. "No, you won't get in trouble. In fact, I really think you should sue your boss, there's gotta be some law against what he did." I stick my tongue out like a child in Jordan's direction. It gets a little smirk out of him.

"You're on. Tomorrow? We could go to the bowling alley on 2nd? Seven?"

I smile, which makes me a horrible person, because I'm smiling at making someone who's grandma is in the hospital upset. "I'll see you there."

I lower the phone into my pocket again and look back in Jordan's direction. He's gone.

"Crap, crap, I am a horrible human I deserve no love."

Russ and Laura look in my direction as I angrily condemn myself. They go back to their previous conversation when I take off looking for Jordan.

This is what I always do with friendships. It's why I'm only friends with two people. I can't seem to make them stay. I always do something that drives them off, or upsets them to the point that they no longer talk to me. I prayed that what I just did wouldn't make Jordan stop talking to me.

I found Jordan halfway down a hall right off the waiting room.

"I'm so sorry, I was just upset, you didn't deserve that." I'm somewhat out of breath as I jog to his side. I place my hands on my knees dramatically huffing air in and out of my lungs.

He's standing in front of a vending machine, watching his drink dispense in front of him. "We seem to be apologizing to each other a lot more than friends should."

My heart smiles somehow at this statement. "Friends? We're friends?" I place my hands on my heart and give a sarcastic gleam in my eyes.

"Wipe that smile off your face. I said we fight more than friends do, that doesn't mean anything." He's grinning from ear to ear when he pulls the drink from the bottom of the machine.

"Diet Coke? Have I turned you? Am I that bad of an influence on *the* Mr. Jordan Myers?" the most wild of smiles appearing on my face.

He promptly hands me the drink while he makes another selection.

"Water, of course." I roll my eyes in the most sarcastic way possible to let him know I'm joking.

Once the water has reached the bottom of the vending machine he reaches in, pulls it out and starts walking back in the direction of the waiting room where all of our friends are at. I walk beside him for a while, before I decide I can't take the silence.

"You know, people who aren't friends don't buy each other Diet Cokes." I bump into him physically with the words.

All he can do is chuckle, but not give a full laugh. I continue talking, since it is quite obvious that he isn't going to speak first.

By the time we reach the end of the hallway, I pull my hand out of my pocket and grab his bare forearm. He must have taken off his suit and rolled up his sleeves without my noticing, although I don't know how I didn't notice his forearms. We come to a complete stop, and I almost force him to look in my direction.

"I'm really sorry about your grandmother. She always brought me cookies and took care of me."

He gives a half smile, almost like he's won a competition. "You said grandmother."

I hit his chest, almost making the capless bottle of Diet Coke spill. "I did not!" I refuse.

"Did too, and it was cute."

There goes my stomach again with those butterflies, I'm starting to think they can stick around. We both continue into the waiting room with our eyes glued to the ground. We won't stop looking at each other if we look now, and I think both of us know that.

We go to our unassigned seats against the wall and keep doing what we do best in this room. We wait.

"The family of Georgia Hidi?" A man in business attire and a long white coat walks out into the room, which somehow feels significantly smaller than before.

I pinch the side of Jordan's arm, signaling him to move. I could tell he was frozen. Anik slowly rises from the chair he finally settled in and Jordan goes to grab his arm to help him over.

Once the two are conversing with the doctor, I walk over to Russ and Laura and sit across from them in an empty chair.

"I can't believe this is happening." I rub my eyes with my elbows planted to my knees.

"What were you doing with Jordan just now?"

I look up with so much disdain in my eyes that I feel like the whole room felt the shift in tone. I stand up and start yelling in a whisper. "That's what you want to talk about? Me and Jordan? Are you kidding me right now?" I couldn't believe this was happening.

I didn't even let him finish what he was saying. I walked to the opposite side of the waiting room and sat with my arms crossed, glancing every so often at the couple that I once considered friends.

Me and Russ have only fought once in our lives since becoming friends. We bickered every once and a while, but never raised our voices until our senior year. Russ had tried to set me up with some guy for prom, and he knew how I felt about crowds and well… people in general. The guy showed up to my door and I left him in tears…Looking back, I feel a little guilty. Russ was only trying to get me out there, but I didn't let him.

This fight or whatever this was with Russ felt like something much bigger, like it was years in the making.

"Hey." Jordan sluffs into the seat next to me.

"Hi. What happened?" We meet our eyes, and he seems a little more hopeful than the past hour and a half.

"She had a minor heart attack. It usually goes unnoticed, but because of her age it took a toll. They're keeping her for observations, but will send her to a cardiologist for further testing." He spoke extremely quickly, almost like he couldn't decide if the news was good or bad.

I shake my head in the happiest sad manner possible. I was glad she was going to be ok, but sad at the position she was in.

"Can I ask you a question?" My voice trails, but I get the nod of approval from Jordan. "I haven't met anyone as close as you are to your grandparents. I mean, I was close with mine, but once I grew up, I guess I slowly stopped seeing them, except for holidays."

Jordan examines the room, thinking thoroughly through the question I just threw at him. He grabs my wrist, making the cross unfurl and pulls me up.

"Come on. I'll tell you, but I don't want your pals listening." He nods towards the two in the corner.

We were far enough away from Russ and Laura that they couldn't have possibly heard anything, but I understand the need for privacy.

He leads me to the end of what seems like the record holding, longest hallway around. We enter a room that says 'Family Bereavement Room' . This room is small, but comfortable. A completely different feeling than the rest of the hospital. We sit across from each other on separate couches and stare. Jordan finally drops his gaze and pulls his elbows to his knees and crosses his fingers to keep them still.

"My parents were forty-eight when they had me. I was a surprise, they didn't want any children, and to have one so late was more of an inconvenience than a blessing." He shifts to meet my eyes and drops his crossed fingers in between his legs. "My dad had a really nice job, and they were supposed to retire at fifty. Now it's not much of a retirement when taking care of a two-year-old. So, they bought a home somewhere in Malibu, handed me off to my grandparents and left. It was pretty simple."

My eyes burn, but I don't let the tears fall. "But your last name…Myers…is that?"

"My parents. I kept their last name. My grandparents thought that if they got to keep me, that my parents should at least have the name to prove that I was theirs. I was going to change it at some point, but did you know that costs money? I don't wanna spend a dime on them, especially because it's not going to change a single thing."

My mouth drops, and I have to force myself shut it despite the complete shock I'm in. "I can't believe that. They just let you go, just like that?" I gesture at Jordan with one hand, and I receive a nod in return.

"When I left right before eighth grade graduation, it was because they retired, and I had to come with them."

"Wow." It was the only word that could come out of my mouth.

It makes a lot more sense that I actually had a good time at graduation. My biggest enemy wasn't there, I couldn't remember whether or not I noticed that he wasn't there. I stand up and he matches me.

"I'm so sorry. You didn't deserve that. I would've kept you,

I hope you know that."

"I know that, Annie. I know you would have."

I go in for a hug, but Jordan pushes his hand to the side of my cheek, his thumb right above my ear, the rest covering my face down to my jaw. I inhale sharply, trying not to make it obvious, but the noise could have filled the entire room.

His other hand does the same, my hands still on his chest from my original effort to hug him. I can hear every breath he makes, every breath I make, quickening with every second. I lower my hands to my side in an effort to break free, but this just gives him a window of opportunity. Once my hands are by my side we collide. This doesn't feel like the first time we kissed, this feels blissful, passionate and loving. I never want it to end. I pull my hands from my side and put my hands on his mid back, the most comfortable place my hands have ever been. I attempt to push him in further, but he pulls himself back and scratches the back of his head. My stomach is going crazy with emotion. He had been waiting to do that ever since our last interaction, and the wait was over.

Chapter 7

Unexpected Reunion

We distance ourselves to the opposite ends of the room in an attempt to keep our composure with our bodies. Somehow, with butterflies in my stomach, I manage my way to the other side of the room, passing Jordan, and exit without a word. I didn't know what to do, what to think. Jordan follows behind me, also in silence. Once we are back in the waiting room, I grab my things and make my way over to Russ and Laura, hoping they don't detect what just occurred, can someone smell kisses? Is that a thing?

"I'm sorry about Georgia, I'll see you later." I don't turn around as I speak to Jordan, I just make my way to the other side of the room.

"Don't make promises you can't keep Annie." The words ring in my ears. Annie, no one but him calls me Annie, and at this point I don't think I would allow anyone else to call me by that name.

While I wouldn't normally go home with people when I don't know the stance of our relationship, even more than my anger towards Russ, I don't trust myself in a car alone with Jordan.

We don't speak the entire way home, and I have to force myself to act naturally in their back seat, wiping a grin every few seconds as I recollect those moments.

Arriving at our apartment complex, I take the stairs to avoid an awkward elevator ride with them. I don't know what they have going on right now, but I am not letting it ruin my night. I open my door and realize I'm holding the key that Jace made me. If I wasn't a bad person before for making that phone call in front of Jordan, I'm sure bad now. I decide I should handle it now rather than later, even if Jordan and I don't date, it's not fair to string him along for the ride.

The phone rings in my ear as I wait for him to pick up.

"Hello?" His voice is disheveled and deeper than usual.

I look at the clock. Past midnight. "Oh my gosh, I'm so sorry I didn't realize what time it was." Waking him up in the middle of the night definitely makes me a worse person than before.

"Don't worry about it, are you ok?"

His concern makes it harder than I thought to say what I say next. "I'm fine, I just… I don't think it's a good idea to go out. I was hoping we could just be friends instead. I'm so sorry."

He sighs at my remarks. I crushed him, good going.

"No need to apologize, you checked something off my list." A good attitude makes it slightly easier to end things.

"What did I check off, Mr. Locksmith?"

All I can imagine right now is a pen crossing over, *crazy lady leads me on and then dumps me all within a month.*

"Heartbreak."

I feel so bad. Jace is probably one of the best people I know, but I knew it was wrong to do what I did.

"Goodnight, Anna." He hangs up the phone before I'm able to say anything in return.

Disappointed in myself, I make my way to my room and peel off my layers to reveal a tank top and boxers. Boxers were way more comfortable than what society tells me I should wear. I fall asleep and wake up to my phone's text tone. Jordan had messaged me.

Hey are you going to this?
   Download image

It was a picture of the envelope for our eighth grade reunion. Truth be told I didn't know if I was going to it. I felt like there wasn't a point with Russ not going, and especially since Russ and I aren't even talking right now.

I don't know, I haven't thought about it much

Come with me.

What?

Come with me, please.

You want me to come with you? Why?

You know why. Please don't make me go alone.

I'll meet you there.

Perfect. As always.

I held my phone to my chest and my butterflies arrived again. I went and opened the letter to confirm the dates I had seen in the picture Jordan sent me. August 17th, 2019. Two days after my birthday. At least I got to squeeze that in before facing all these people.

Another week went by of not talking to Russ and Laura. This was the time we had deliberately not spoken for as long as I can remember. There were many times throughout the week where I felt like calling, but didn't. I was as much to blame as they were; it was just a decision of who would break first. My birthday was coming up this Thursday and would be the first time since eighth grade I didn't celebrate with him. It felt like a big joke.

I know that Russ didn't like Jordan, but he never really told me why. I don't understand why he would take it this far. To be fair, I had also been ignoring Russ and Laura, but I had a reason to be mad: they were treating me horribly because of a person.

It felt weird to just call Jordan a person. He was who I confided in now, he felt like so much more.

I didn't go over to their house last week for any of our usual dedicated hangouts. It felt like I couldn't after what had happened. Still, I felt like I was missing someone, and I knew exactly who it was.

I decided, despite my regular amount of laziness, that I should take a walk and clear my head. Once I slip my barely used running shoes on and grab my headphones, I head out the door. There is a letter sitting on the edge of the frame. It was a reused envelope from Russ and Laura's apartment. I was terrified to open it; for all I knew, this was an official letter to tell me we weren't friends anymore. I opened the letter after taking out my right earbud. It was a newly made invitation for my birthday party. My heart leaped with happiness knowing that our friendship hadn't been declared over. Russ threw me a party every year. He knew I didn't want to see many people, so he called it a party, made an invitation, and just had it be Russ, Laura and I. He made it comfortable to celebrate, and that was something I could count on.

I sent a picture to Jordan of the invitation and called him immediately after.

"Did you get my text?" I'm whispering as I sit down back on my couch. I decide a run is no longer necessary. Thank goodness.

"You mean the one that just came through? Yeah, I got it." I can hear a smile creeping onto his lips through the speaker.

"Will you come? For me? For poor ole Annabelle?"

He sighs, and I imagine his smile disappears.

"Please?" I make puppy dog eyes to myself and beg.

"Oh alright, but only because I'm making you go to this reunion thing." His smile returns.

"Perfect, I'll see you here at seven, Thursday." I hang up the phone so he doesn't have a chance to change his mind.

The next twenty-three hours I spend almost constantly on the phone with Jordan. We talk about how his grandma is doing, and our childhoods, and how I can't believe I ever hated him.

"So, is she doing ok now?"

We had just finished talking about how his grandma had been released from the hospital.

"She's alright. Her diet is very strict right now which is driving her up the wall. She's always been the person who brings and eats the cookies, and now she's stuck with broccoli and low cholesterol foods." His voice is strained; I think he knows that her changing her diet meant no more cookies for him.

"Hey Jordan?" My voice trails.

"Mhm? What's up?" It has such a casual tone.

"I don't mind talking to you. I think you're the only person who I see calling me that doesn't send me into a panic." I can almost picture him sprawled on his couch phone on speaker, just watching the hours climb.

"That is probably the most flattering thing anyone has ever said to me."

"Shut up." I walked over to the kitchen and started making dinner. Five hours had passed while on the phone with Jordan. I didn't think I could enjoy a person so much, especially since…well, since I hate people.

Thursday approaches and I'm starting to get nervous throughout the day. Is this some prank? Am I going to show up all dressed for nothing? Jordan reminds me a few times that everything will be ok, and I try to believe him, but it becomes increasingly difficult the closer we get. Throughout the past few days, I've started to welcome the butterflies I once tried to get rid of. I don't really want them there, but I guess they can stay while they're in town.

Seven creeps closer towards me and I make myself get ready. I put on my deep green dress, makeup and curl my hair. Every year we dress up for my birthday. I don't get many opportunities throughout the rest of the year, so this is always my one and only excuse.

Hard knocking encompasses my door and I go to it quicker than usual. I throw the door open and almost slam it into the wall.

"Hi." Jordan smiles and with that smile, the one that drives me insane. He's propping himself on the doorway with his elbow, both hands in his suit pockets as usual. "Woah, you look…just woah." He looks me up and down as he examines my floor length dress.

I tuck the right side of my hair behind my ear and look to the ground, blushing more than before. This time I let the warmth hug me as I embrace how Jordan makes me feel.

"Thanks, you look nice, as always," I say, still looking at the ground. I try not to let out the most movie-like giggle as I say the words.

Jordan holds out his elbow for me to grasp, and I take it with my left hand, feeling his bicep through the suit jacket. We both make our way to the elevator and make our way up to the fourth floor.

"You guys should really get this thing checked," he laughs as the elevator drops while making its stop.

"It makes this place homey," I laugh at his comment.

My stomach starts turning in an unpleasant way once we reach the fourth floor. Instinctively, I tighten my grip on Jordans arm.

"Ouch. You okay?" Jordan slightly lifts his arm once my grip tightens and I find myself in a hazy fog.

My breathing feels shallow, and the rest of my body feels like it is going limp, almost like I am losing control of both my mind and body. Jordan unhooks his arm from mine and pulls me out of the closing elevator doors, forcing them to reopen since I was in the way. His feet keep moving but the rest of my body stops.

I start panicking, almost like I'm about to walk into some type of death trap. Warmth wakes me from this illusion I have put myself in, and once both my mind and body are back, I realize that it's Jordan's hands over both of my cheeks, forcing my eyes to his. If I wasn't in some kind of illusion before, Jordan's eyes hypnotize me now. His thumbs rest at the highest point of my cheekbones and rub my face to soothe my anxiety. Lips that I know all too well at this point press against my forehead, and I feel myself leaning into their comfort and familiarity.

"What happened? I know that you guys fought, but what happened?" his voice growls in a whisper, demanding to know the answer, but I know I won't give it.

Now is not the time to try and explain to him that they hate him for unknown reasons. They may have had an excuse when we were still in school, but those excuses are long gone at this point.

"I'm fine, really, I just needed a minute. Let's go." Speaking in a soft whisper, I break from his inviting clutch and make my way towards their apartment door. Jordan follows next to me and he slides his hand against the green fabric laying on my back.

Once we arrive, I lift a fist to knock on the door, but freeze while in motion. Jordan somehow gets the hint and knocks himself, while I put my hands together in front of me. I can hear footsteps inside, and small voices make sounds, what seems like bickering, but I can't quite discern the voices.

The door opens and Laura is at the door. I don't know why this makes me inhale a sharp breath, but it does. I can't tell who I am more mad at, Laura or Russ. Laura knows the problem, but won't tell me the whole situation, and Russ is being well… he's being a jerk.

Without a single word, Laura moves out of the way and holds her arm out in signal to come in. Guided by Jordan's hand, I walk through the door and my anxiety quickly heightens when I'm bombarded with surrounding shouts.

"Surprise!" My entire family pops out from behind couches and kitchen counters and even my younger brother pops out from behind a curtain.

I try to put on my most convincing happy face, but can feel that it isn't all that convincing after all.

Both of my parents come out from their hiding spots and start making their way toward me. In normal situations people would expect a hug, but not in this family. We just acknowledge each other's presence awkwardly, and call it good.

"Happy birthday!" My mom is shouting as she walks towards me in a fitted red dress.

My dad raises a glass of what I assume is sprite since he doesn't drink, that was his way of agreeing with the sentiment of my mother's words.

"Mom…Dad!" My voice fluctuates and I hope they can't tell that this wasn't really what I would consider a party.

Jordan immediately drops his hand from my back, and I am more grateful than he knows. My parents and I try to talk often, but the last thing I would want to talk to them about is my love life…or whatever this thing with Jordan is. I see my mother's gaze drop to Jordan's hand as it falls to his side, but I am relieved when she doesn't acknowledge it.

Once we get over the surprise that is the rest of my family showing up, I start making my rounds. My aunt Rachael is here; we don't talk often, so seeing her is a surprise. She's one of the people in your family that gets way too invested in your personal business.

"Ok, I am really hoping I saw correctly, because that man is MMM."

I put my hand to her wrist as she gestures towards Jordan. "Stop that, he's just an old friend…or something. He's having me go to a reunion with him, so I dragged him here in return."

She simply takes a sip of her drink and nods before walking away.

Within seconds, Jordan grabs my hand at my side and pulls me into Laura's home office. "Woah, you did not tell me your whole family was going to be here."

I free my hand from him. "I didn't know they were going to be here. I just told you last night how judgmental they are, do you think I would parade around a boy with them around?"

Jordan scratches his nape and looks at me. "You're right, I'm sorry. It just threw me a little is all."

"Right back atcha."

I tell Jordan to stay in the room for a minute. The last thing I need is for Rachael to think we were in here by ourselves. Once I make my way fully out of the room, I see her staring directly at me giving me a sly nod and wink. I shake my head in disapproval, but I don't think she really got the message. She gives Jordan the same look once he exits.

Throughout the night, Russ and I make awkward eye contact, but not a word is spoken. Jordan somehow keeps his distance for the remainder of the party, but always remains in sight as we mingle with my family, and a few family friends who I don't know very well.

Jordan and I make eye contact as he talks to my little brother, and I am making conversation with another person who lives on the fourth floor.

"I'm sorry," I mouth the words in his direction, and I can see him try and contain his smile. We go back to our conversations, and continue with the next hour.

It takes everything in me to not kick everyone out. My nerves slowly climb, and I become extremely grateful once the music stops and everyone seems to be slowly separating.

Everyone starts making their way out the door, and somehow I end up being the person standing at the door saying goodbyes, instead of the hosts.

"It was nice to see you, Mom, we need to see each other more often."

My mom touches my arm and pulls me in a little to whisper slightly. "Who is that?" She starts to point in Jordan's direction, but I quickly put her hand down before he notices.

"His name is Jordan, he's the owner of Castinos." I try not to give too much away.

Sure…that's all he is, just the owner of the hotel across town. Convincing myself doesn't work very well, but I hope it makes her understand I don't want any further questions. She luckily takes the hint and follows my brother and father into the hallway as I shut the door and take a deep breath.

"That was fun." Jordan is almost giggling at my expression.

"Not funny. I didn't know they were going to be here, otherwise I wouldn't have brought a douche canoe." My grin takes over half my face and Jordan's smile matches mine. Finally, I make my way over to him, we don't touch, but having him near me makes me feel better.

"Douche canoe is right." Russ appears from the bedroom and takes a sip of his Dr. Pepper, his drink of choice, always.

I turn to scowl at him. Now is not the time or place for some prophetic fight.

"What? What did you say?" Jordan takes a step towards Russ leaving me to myself, while Laura watches from the kitchen.

"We should really get going. It was so much fun, thank you both." I grab Jordan by the hand, but he pulls it away, leaving my hand feeling cold.

"Listen, I don't know what you have against me, but you don't get to take it out on Annie, just because she has decided that I can be her…her friend."

The word friend stabs me in the chest. Is that what this is? Friendship? I feel my throat begin to tighten the closer they get. For all I know, Jordan is about to punch Russ, in a way more violent way than Jace.

Russ looks towards me and then back at Jordan. "Her name

is Anna. And I'm not mad at her for whatever you guys have going on, I'm mad at her for being stupid enough to not see through your crap."

I can see both of their faces begin to brighten with red in anger. Laura and I exchange glances, not knowing what to do.

"Don't call her stupid." I have never heard Jordan's voice this low, but it sounds like a rumble throughout the apartment.

"Why not? You're both stupid. She's stupid for talking to you, and you've been stupid since eighth grade. You were so into her you would do anything to be near her." Russ is throwing his arms, pointing between me and Jordan.

His statement makes me take another quick inhale, and makes my future breaths become the same ones I experienced in the elevator.

"What?" I finally speak up, since the beginning of the argument.

Jordan looks at me and then angrily looks back at Russ. "You have no clue what you're talking about, shut up." Jordan's eyes begin to light with fire, his anger turning to rage.

"What, so she doesn't know?" Russ looks from Jordan to me, and I can't quite tell if he wants an answer. "Jordan didn't go around doing all that stuff to you in eighth grade, it was me. I had a giant crush on you, and when I found out Jordan also liked you, I got angry, so I said all those things at the dance, and blamed them on Jordan. He never told anyone the truth because you being mad at him meant that you would constantly talk to him, whether you were being mean or not. It was all a ploy to get you to pay attention to him."

My mouth drops, and I turn my glance to Jordan. "Is that true?"

He only shamefully nods in response. Keeping his head

down.

I start grabbing my things and head for the door.

"Wait!" both of them yell at me in unison.

"Wait? Are you kidding me?" I continue on my way. My voice unintentionally raises.

"See what you did, Jordan? You always screw things up for her."

I stop in my tracks. There is no way that Russ just tried to gloss over the fact that he lied to me too.

"You do not get off scot-free, Russ. You lied to me. Not only did you lie to me, you were the one who did all that stuff to me. I was miserable. You watched me be miserable." I can feel my cool tears running down my hot face.

"Let's go, Annie."

"And you, I told you all about how much I hated you in eighth grade for what you did, and you said nothing, not a word. Don't act like you're innocent either." I can feel my voice changing the more I speak. I don't get angry often, but when I do it always ends up with me crying and running out usually before my piece is done. This time I wasn't going to let it go.

Both of them stop speaking as they see my face change. "Laura, you didn't do anything, but you could have told me. You should have told me." My anger is slowly turning into sadness.

"Come on, you know me, I wouldn't do that again, and I know you, you can forgive us for this, it was ten years ago." Jordan starts pleading with me, but I can't even think about that right now.

"I know you? Sure I do, you're the same douche canoe I knew ten years ago. And you have no clue who I am, our conversations last night don't mean that you *know* me. I've changed since eighth grade. I'm not some girl you can tease on at lunch and recess and think that will make me pay attention to you. You have no clue who I am anymore."

I hear them say something to me, but I can't make it out. My ears are ringing with fury. I walk out the door and slam it as hard as possible. Halfway down the hall I find myself sobbing. I've been doing that a lot since I met Jordan. The butterflies I just felt were not the butterflies I had grown accustomed to, these were angry and vengeful butterflies.

Mr. Hidi is standing at the end of the hall, waiting for the elevator, smiling and waving at me. I find myself going to the staircase. I don't want to take out any anger on him just because he's related to him.

Once I'm down the stairs I run to my door, blinking the blurry wetness out of my eyes. My hands shake violently as I try and turn the knob. Frustrated, I throw my keys on the ground and I have to stop myself from leaving the building all together. It takes me a few tries but I finally get my door open and race inside, throwing my things onto my counter. I let out loud grunts over and over again as things don't go my way.

Everything on my body felt like it was suffocating me; I couldn't breathe. I run to my room and quickly but forcefully took my makeup off. I can't believe I put mascara on for this guy. The tears help the makeup come off more easily.

I run over to my drawers and throw a shirt and leggings on the bed. I struggle trying to get the zipper off, but I eventually make due. Once I'm in my comfortable clothes, I hide under my covers and finally let the sobs fall. Harder than I wanted to admit to myself. I had a few tears throughout the fighting, but these were continuous streams that left my pillow case soaked.

Chapter 8

Road Trip

Over the next day I received many texts from both Jordan and Russ, almost begging me for forgiveness, but I chose to ignore all of them. Although I am twenty-three now, the pain that I encountered during school still lingers. I was miserable, I didn't experience high school like most girls because I tucked myself into my own corner and avoided everyone. They stole that from me, if they were just honest I could have had a boyfriend, and a best friend, and life would have been great.

Most of the messages read "Call me," or something like that, but I couldn't handle hearing their voices right now. It would only make me go back to that place of pure anger.

I picked up a few hours at work to try and take my mind off things. I wanted to focus on anything but the men in my life, both of them. I wasn't going to work this Saturday so I had taken the time off for the reunion, but since I'm not doing anything anymore, I decided the money wouldn't hurt.

After I finished my shift, I let my boss know about another infidelity in someone's projections. I shouldn't think this, but it felt good to give bad news instead of being on the opposite end of things.

Numbers were good, I could do numbers. People, on the other hand, I can't do, not right now at least. I close my laptop and head back over to the kitchen to make a quick meal. I spot the luggage I had packed in preparation for tomorrow, and I get a twinge.

"You know what, I'm going to go," I tell myself matter-of-factly as I wait for my mac and cheese to finish in the microwave. I am going to go, and I won't let anyone stand in my way. I realized that I don't eat much good food without Russ and Laura, but at least I was eating. I had bad habits when I was stressed in the past, so I'll take the mac and cheese.

I have been watching reruns of Spongebob over the past twenty-three hours, trying to comfort myself and when it finally reaches midnight I decide it's time to turn in. I clean the bowls I had in the sink from my mac and cheese and ice cream, and the minute I finish I head towards my room. Once I hit my pillow, I fell asleep instantaneously. I didn't realize that the amount of emotional turmoil that I have encountered in the past few weeks had made me so exhausted. The dreams I had that night were mainly violent ones toward men. They suck. At least the ones in my life right now suck.

The ring of my alarm wakes me up at seven a.m. It was a custom tone that Jordan had helped me figure out how to install it. Donny Osmond's 'Will it Go Round in Circles' plays and I shut it off before the main chorus. I would usually let it play while I got ready, but I didn't feel like dancing today.

I rub the crust off my eyes that had formed due to my tears with a warm washcloth that steamed as it melted away what was on my face. I didn't want to look awful this afternoon, and this was my first step in hopefully avoiding that.

The reunion was at two, but it was about five hours away, and I needed to make it in time to check into the hotel I booked last night. My original plan was to go stay at a local Hard Rock, but I wasn't able to make any reservations when Jordan had asked me to come with him. I was playing on winging it, but the thought made me nervous last night that I would potentially have to sleep in my car if I couldn't find anything in time. No way with my luck would I find another cute hotel owner to let me stay the night. I switch from my shirt and leggings to an old Hard Rock sweatshirt and a pair of plain denim jeans and check to make sure I look ok enough to go into gas stations.

I stop at the mirror in front of my door, and move my side braid a little. "Ok, you've got this." I glare at myself in the mirror, trying to fully convince myself of the lie I just told.

I go to reach for my door when I hear a knock. My hand jerks from the knob.

"Who is it?" I say, a little louder than necessary.

"Annie, please. You promised. You pinky promised at the hospital." The all-familiar voice makes an echo through my ears.

Curse me and my pinky promise. I wish I didn't take those so seriously. They always seem to bite me in the butt. I open the door slightly, but the chain remains, leaving a gap large enough that I can see him. I want to cry as I open the door.

I have never seen Jordan like this. He was wearing loose jeans and a Hard Rock shirt from Boise. I catch myself staring at the shirt.

"I drove three hours just to get this. I thought it would be fitting."

A smile encroaches onto my face, but I immediately swipe it as I realize who I'm talking to.

"You wouldn't break a pinky promise, would you?" He reaches out a pinky in my direction.

I roll my eyes and lock his pinky with mine through the door. Pinky promises are like silent vows.

I shut the door once our hands lower and unlock the latch.

"I'm not talking to you. So let's just skip the small talk." I cross my arms over my chest keeping myself physically closed off from him.

He mimics a zipper going over his mouth and nods.

I can't believe I'm doing this, but I have never broken a pinky promise and don't plan on starting now. Not at the hands of him.

We get into his car, his stupid shiny new model car, and I start lifting my luggage before he grabs it from my grasp and sets it into the trunk. I have decided I hate chivalry. Especially when it comes from Jordan. Protesting would mean breaking my silence though.

Once I am fully satisfied with my position in the passenger seat, I see Jordan come around the car from the trunk. He pulls his door open and sluffs into the front seat.

"You could've at least let me open the door for you."

Again, I hate chivalry. I look at him and make the imaginary zipper appear on my mouth now, sliding my fingertips across my lips slowly. He watches every move they make, centimeter by centimeter. Noticing him watching my hand, or was he watching my lips? I push my hand down and pick at both hands with my nails. I did this often when I was anxious. I've been told that it's normal, but these little things I do make me feel like I'm the odd one out sometimes.

I keep my stare towards the windshield as Jordan begins to back up. He puts his hand on the back of my seat and my eyes start wandering towards his arm. I see him watching my eyes, noticing the trail they are leaving behind, and he puts the car back in park and looks at me.

"Annie, if you keep looking at me like that we aren't going to get anywhere." He's breathless with his words.

To be fair, I wasn't really looking at him as a whole, I was looking at a specific appendage. Okay that is also a lie, my eyes were tracing a very particular vein that crawls from his wrist to his elbow and then disappears.

"I'm sorry, continue with your driving." I look back at my hands. I've almost picked them raw, and I can start feeling the pulses that linger below my fingertips.

I examine my nails when I feel his deep dark mud eyes on the tips of my hand. He puts his hand over both of mine. No man should ever have hands that are able to encompass both hands of another person.

"Stop that, you're driving me nuts, and your hands are paying for it."

He's right, my hands are paying for it, and I somehow hope I'm driving him nuts. After all he pulled, he deserves it.

We make it out of town and hop on the freeway. I'm really stuck in this car now. I might have been able to tuck and roll in town, but I can't do that when we're going nearly eighty down the roads.

His hands haven't moved from mine since we pulled out. His touch makes my heart flutter, but if I had my way, I would get them off of me. I don't need to be watched, me or my fingers. I just can't seem to find the strength to move his enormous hands.

By the time we're out of the county, the radio is playing Donny Osmond and I'm singing along in my head. Normally I would be singing my heart out, but I did not need to be made fun of by him. He had done enough already.

I reach my hand to skip over a song that I have overplayed to the point that I don't think I'll be able to play it anymore for the rest of my lifetime. I was able to free my hands from his clutch about ten minutes ago.

Jordan grabs my hand again, right before I press the skip button. He is really good at grabbing my hands at inopportune times.

"Annabelle, I am so sorry." The entire mood shifts in the car, I feel my eyes become hot, but I don't allow anything to spill.

Here we go. I was hoping we could avoid this despite being in a car for five hours together, but I guess I should've known better.

"Don't start. Please. I just wanted to skip this song and get on our way." My voice becomes irritated, and my angry butterflies return as I remember all the has happened in the past seventy-two hours.

"No, listen." He interrupts me. "First of all, I just want to say that I thought Russ would have told you by now." The list of excuses begins, but it shouldn't have been up to Russ to tell me, he should have told me. "When he started yelling at me at your birthday party, I realized he hadn't, and I felt like an idiot. Please, you have to believe that I wouldn't do that."

Silence overwhelms us both. I think he's looking for a response, but I know I won't say anything nice right now. I need a minute to process what he has said. Maybe he really wouldn't do something like that to me now, but it still stung my heart that it happened at all.

Jordan eventually drops my hand and it takes me fifteen minutes to finally speak up, but all that comes out is "I have to pee." I don't know if I've forgiven him yet, but we're getting somewhere.

We pull over at the next exit and bring the car to a stop at the gas pump.

"I'll get gas, you go in and…well, pee. When you get back, I'll go in and we'll switch."

I nod in agreement, and without another word I hop out of his car and make my way into the sloppy gas station.

"Bathrooms?" I ask as I pass an attendant stocking the chips in an aisle.

"To the left." The older lady points in that direction and I smile in gratitude.

I go to the bathroom, but instead of actually peeing I run water over my face to cool myself down. I remove the heavy sweatshirt off of my body and reveal a deep purple tank top underneath, and stare at myself in the mirror. I watch the green appear on my face and scurry to the nearby stall.

Nothing comes up, but my stomach is twisting and turning in the most nauseating way possible. Despite my best efforts to avoid it, Jordan Myers knows how to apologize, the type of apology written by a woman.

I can't tell if my stomach is feeling this way due to the forsaken creatures in there, or if I was actually sick. Either way, I don't want this feeling to continue. I have to push my feelings or butterflies, or whatever you want to call them aside. Once I get past this reunion, it will all go back to normal.

Making my way back to the car I see a penny on the ground. Most people think that pennies are good luck, but it felt like I could use anything that was deemed good luck right now. I avoid broken mirrors, try to avoid sidewalk cracks, and more.

A family passes me as I walk into the open part of the parking lot. A little kid is running inside, telling his mom he scraped his knee. I get down on both my knees as he approaches me.

"Here, take this, it's good luck." I handed him the penny I had just picked off the asphalt.

He begins this huge smile and takes off shouting at his mom

that he's all better now.

I laugh at myself a little. I love how simple kids are. It's one of the reasons I want to be a teacher. They don't need anything complicated to be happy, just someone that cares. And I desperately wanted to be the person that cared for them.

I straightened myself, wiped off my jeans and looked towards the car. Jordan is watching me and grinning from ear to ear. I smile back, before stopping myself. I'm supposed to be mad at him. It is so hard to be mad at him.

Once I reach the car, I stay with the gas tank, and watch Jordan switch with me and start racing inside.

"You can do this, you can be mad at someone. You can not like Jordan, it is possible." Pep talks are something I have to give to myself often, I just didn't think I would ever give myself a pep talk about how I needed to hate someone. Life is weird sometimes.

Emotions are something I have always had a hard time with. I'm a well-known people pleaser; it feels like I break inside every time I utter the word 'no'. I was always the employee to sign up for extra hours, to show up early to parties to help set up, the person everyone knew they could count on. The problem with that is I would always help other people before I helped myself. I so desperately wanted to be selfish for once.

The past weeks flash before my eyes when I see him come back from the bathrooms. Every touch, every look, every kiss. Every time we kiss there have been some kind of repercussions, people have gotten angry, hurt, that's what I'll focus on, that's what will keep me angry with him.

Once he makes his way towards the gas tank, I start walking towards the passenger side of the car and climb in. The more I avoid being close to him, the better.

Jordan sits himself next to me after unhooking the hose from the car. Crinkling of a white generic bag sitting on his lap starts to fill my ears. I didn't even realize he had something in his hand when he was walking toward me earlier.

"Here you go, I figured if we were in it for a while, we might as well have some snacks." Jordan pulls out a Diet Coke and a bag of Gushers from the white bag.

I understand the Diet Coke, but how on earth did he know about the Gushers? A thought pops into my mind. He takes care of me, not that I can count a bag of basically sugar really taking care of me.

Once they are in my hands, I look at them, almost with examining eyes.

"I forgive you." The words come out of my mouth without permission.

"If I had known all it took was some high fructose corn syrup and carbonation I would have been at your house in an hour after your party." Jordan speaks through his smile.

I have failed my mission. I can't stay mad at him despite my best efforts.

"How did you know about the Gushers? I never told you my favorite snack was Gushers," I laugh as I start opening the yellow package filled with the sweet liquid filled fruit snacks.

"The wrappers. I saw a few wrappers in your bag when you stayed at Castino's and then I saw some at your house on the counter when I picked you up. It was more of a guesstimation to be honest."

The only thing that went through my head was that he pays attention to every detail, even my trash. I shouldn't be so happy about someone paying attention to my trash, but I am.

My soda hisses as I begin to open it in an attempt to wash

the sticky substance from my mouth.

"I can't believe how much Diet Coke you drink, at this point you should be hooked up to an I.V."

I can stand a car ride with him, but I will not stand for Diet Coke slander.

"Try it, have you ever even had it?" I tip my bottle towards him as he restarts the ignition.

"I've only had caffeine-free soda, none of this…bottled death." He's flicking his fingers at the bottle and starts to drive back towards the freeway.

"Come on, for me?" I flick my eyes even though I know he isn't watching.

The Diet Coke gets placed into the cup holder next to me and I screw the lid on as I beg for him to try it, just one sip.

"Fine. One sip." I've finally broken him down I get to watch Jordan Myers have his first taste of caffeine. This can be my revenge.

Suddenly he slams on the breaks. A semi has run off the road, causing all traffic to come to a sudden stop. I slide forward a little bit, but I'm stopped by his arm. He had flung it out in front of my chest in an attempt to make sure I stayed in my seat.

"Did… did you just mom arm me?" This was something my mother did frequently when we were kids. She wasn't the best driver.

"Did I just what now?" Jordan raises an eyebrow as we wait for the traffic to start moving again.

"Mom arm me. Something that moms do to protect their kids from flying all over the place." I try and explain to him, but he seems more confused than before. I forgot he didn't grow up with his mom. "I'm sorry I… I forgot." I regret my decision to explain.

"No…no it has nothing to do with my parents, I've just never heard of that term before." Jordan tries to reassure me, but I have a hard time believing I didn't do anything wrong. I seem to do wrong things all the time.

"Ok back to business Diet Coke." I reach for the bottle and my hand hits the lid and Jordan's hand lays on mine. We tried to grab the bottle at the same time. His mere touch sends me into a hypnotic spiral.

The butterflies are back, and they are back bigger than before. I am not a bold person, but I seem to be my most courageous version of myself around this man.

"Kiss me." The words escape my mouth in an almost whisper. I can feel my chest raising with each breath as I watch Jordan's face come towards mine. He gave me no time to actually prepare for him to kiss me, even though I was the one who asked. I close my eyes in anticipation, but all I feel is hot words against my ear lobe.

"Not in a million years Annabelle."

My ears ring echoing the words he just said, he leans back smiling to himself at what he just said.

"What?" I say with an unknown intention. My eyes shoot open.

"I don't know if you've noticed, but when we kiss people tend to be upset. Kira even got upset when I kissed you at Castino's because I wasn't able to make you stay. Then when I kissed you at the hospital, Russ was pissed off like he always is when I'm around. I want to, trust me, but I also don't think I can handle seeing people be mean to you anymore. It hurts to watch."

I can't believe what he is saying. He wants to, but he won't because of other people? That is ridiculous. His reasoning also sent my heart beating fast, he hates when people are mean to me.

"Jordan."

He shifts his gaze back at mine from the stand still traffic.

"There is nobody here to be mad at me but you." My voice is soft, but serious.

I hear him take a sharp inhale, followed by a long exhale. "Well then, I guess I have no excuses." He shifts the car into park, with a line of cars behind us and pulls my face closer to his. "Annabelle Richards, what am I going to do with you?"

Hearing him say my full name makes my heart melt. I love when he calls me Annie, but he is the one and only person I would ever allow to call me whatever he wanted.

We lean into each other, and our lips collide. They almost feel softer than before. I can feel every crevice and line in his lips, and it makes my heart swoon.

"Jordan Delta Myers, what am I going to do with you?" My voice is higher than usual.

We keep our foreheads pressed to each other and only break contact when car horns surround us. The sound sends both of us into a spiral of laughter.

"That isn't fair, you know, you know my middle name when I don't know yours."

I snicker at his discomfort, knowing full well he'll never know my middle name. "That's because I don't have a middle name." I hold out my pinky to express my sincerity. Most people don't believe me when I tell them I don't have a middle name. I have to spend the majority of my time convincing them. One time, I even brought my birth certificate to work so they would leave me alone.

His finger collides with mine as he continues driving. I'm glad I can have someone take silly little things as seriously as I do.

Breaking our concentration, my phone rings again. This is

the third time, just since I've been in the car.

"Answer it. Russ deserves a chance, just like I did."

I never thought I would ever hear Jordan vouching on behalf of Russ, but here we are.

Before I can answer the phone myself, Jordan slides his finger over the answer key, then sucks his finger as if it had made him draw blood.

"Anna? Are you there?" The voice on my phone is dulled before I bring it up to my ear.

I left a slight laugh out before putting the phone up to my ear. "I'm here. What do you want?" Jordan shoots me a glare while I speak. Maybe I should attempt to be nice to him. "I'm sorry, what's up?" I turn the pitch slightly in my voice so he can understand I'm at least trying.

"Anna, I am so sorry. I never meant to hurt you, I just thought that if I teased you a little bit you would like me back, and it never worked so I gave up. Then we met Laura and every day for two years she told me to tell you, but I never did." His voice is so upset I can't help but feel bad for him.

"I know, Russ, it was just a little shocking is all. I didn't think you would have done that to me. You know how I felt at school stuff because of what you did. I forgive you, but I just think we need a little time to ourselves for a while. Thank you for calling."

"You should thank Jordan, he's the one who convinced me to keep trying. I was ready to give up, but he told me to try until you listened. He's a good guy, you know, I think you should really give him a fair chance." It sounded like he didn't really want to say it, but it was the truth.

Jordan vouching for Russ, Russ vouching for Jordan, who would have thought the world would have come to this?

"I'm about to board, but I'm glad we talked, Anna. I'll see

you when you get home, and we can have taco night. Jordan's invited."

I smile at Jordan, and he can tell that knows the conversation went well.

Once I hang up on the phone, I turn my attention back to Jordan.

"You told Russ to apologize?"

His smile creeps on his face. "No, I just told him not to stop apologizing till you listen. He's a good friend is all."

"Well, that good friend invited you to taco night, you should feel extremely flattered." Laughter escapes me. A month ago, I wouldn't have thought I could put these two in the same room, and now they're planning to stuff meat into corn shells together.

We drive for a few more hours before finally pulling into the hotel the reunion is at. Due to the unforeseen stop we are here a little later than I would have liked.

"Jordan, what are we telling people?" My voice is shaky with anxiety due to the time. Being on time was something I bragged about my whole life, so when I wasn't somewhere when I expected to be there, it caused me discomfort.

"What do you mean?" Jordan lifts the hand off of mine that has been there since we kissed.

"I mean, we haven't really gone on enough dates to be official, but I want to go in with you. I mean, what are we telling people?"

"Oh…that." Jordan brushes his hair with his fingertips and then places them in his pockets. "Well, I say if we are going to go in together, we might as well be together. You can tell them all about the hot, successful hotel owner you are with."

I laugh at his remarks about himself. "So, you want to fake date me?" I have to convince myself not to burst out in hysterics.

"Not necessarily. I mean, we have kissed. I just mean to make it seem a little more serious than it currently is."

I should be offended by these words, but I can't blame him. We haven't really gone out on an official date, and even though we have kissed, we haven't put any labels on anything. I can't hold it against him for thinking like that.

"Let's do it." I nod happily in agreement. Any excuse to have Jordan on my arms is an excuse I'll take, although I hope when this is over we do put labels on things. He is right, I would like to tell everyone about my hot successful boyfriend.

I might be changing my mind about chivalry as I watch Jordan grab our bags from the trunk of his car. He lifts them with such ease, despite my need to pack everything in my sight. My bag must be at least thirty pounds. I grab the hoodie from my feet and slip it on as I exit the car, using the door that he has already opened for me.

My hair gets caught in the shirt and as I attempt to pull the braid from the inside. I feel it's weight fall to my left shoulder; Jordan has already helped me pull the hair out. His hand grazed my neck sending a shiver down my spine. We make eye contact for a brief moment. I hope he doesn't notice that he has literally taken my breath away.

"We might as well start now, you know, just in case we run into people who are setting up." His voice is hushed with secrecy.

"You're right, let's go *boyfriend*." The word 'boyfriend' lingers on my lips as he takes his hand and slips it into his front pocket. I can't tell if the taste of the word was something I wanted to continue tasting, or if it was something like ice cream, it was delicious, but you can't taste too much without getting sick.

We both look at each other one more time before heading to the hotel doors. I assume that Jordan got a room for himself when he initially received the invitation. Once we reach the automatic double doors, Jordan takes the hand from his pocket and reaches for mine and grips tightly. Any ounce of anxiety that I had about this reunion washes away. I try not to attach myself to his touch; this is only for show.

Once we reach the lobby, we both check into our separate rooms, Jordan first then I follow.

"What is the dress code for the Wallace reunion?"

The clerk, who looks to be about eighteen years old, motions at a sign near the reception area doors. **Wallace Charter School Reunion-Cocktail/Formal attire required.**

I feel my cheeks warm with embarrassment, how could I have missed such a giant sign? My mind must have been elsewhere. "Thank you." I grab my key card from the counter and turn towards the elevators, Jordan waiting for me.

"You didn't have to wait for me, you know. We could have just waited until we met for the party to pretend." I grab my bag from Jordan's shoulder, my fingertips brushing against his thin shirt.

He lowers himself to my ear. "That wouldn't be any fun, now would it?" The butterflies are back again, leaving my stomach twisting as he grabs my hand and interlocks our fingers as we stride to the elevators.

"I'll see you downstairs in an hour," I say in the open doorway to my room. My fingers begin slipping from his hand unwillingly.

"That's too long." His voice whines as I shut the door and whisper a goodbye through the narrowing gap.

I sink my back to the door until I am sitting on the floor on the other side. "Jordan Myers gives me butterflies." The words trickle from my mouth in an almost giggling fashion.

I decided, since I only have an hour to get ready, I might as well start now. I packed a few options for clothing, since I wasn't sure what the attire was supposed to be. I sift through a pair of jeans and shirt, along with a small black cocktail dress and my pajamas. The last dress I pull out is a deep red dress, almost maroon. The neckline is somehow a deep V and modest at the same time, and the skirt of the dress hugs most of my body, with a little flare at the end of the skirt. It was no green dress, but it was the second best dress I owned.

Hanging my dress on the bathroom doorknob, I sift through my makeup. Most of it was a few years old, and since I didn't wear makeup very often, I hadn't used it in quite some time. I slip the glasses from my face and trade them for contacts, which burn slightly. I'm assuming they're very expired.

I apply a full face of makeup and top it off with a nude lipstick and gloss. I take a few deep breaths and begin a staring contest in the mirror with myself. Since I don't wear makeup often, seeing myself in such a manner throws me slightly, and I have to convince myself I look okay. Taking a brush, I fix the blending on my neck, and decide that I've done enough with my face. Next step is to curl my hair.

Fifteen minutes pass and I finish the section I was working on. I take my wide tooth comb from my bag and run it through my strands a few times loosening the curls until they look perfectly messy. Jewelry was my last step. I added a few silver accents and looked at myself one more time before slipping on my silver heels.

"You've got this." I smile in the mirror one more time before I start heading towards the door. I assumed I would be meeting Jordan in the lobby, but I hear his distinct knocks at my door. I grab my clutch, which has my cards, phone, and lip gloss readily available just in case. I take one more deep breath before I open the door.

My breath stops when my eyes see Jordan's tuxedo. The man wears suits almost constantly, but the way this hugs his body ensures this is custom. His fingers close my mouth, which I haven't realized was gaping open.

"Woah." The words escape me.

"Screw the green dress, you look…you look beautiful."

I look at the ground as he compliments me. Fingers bring my face up towards him and he kisses my cheek, so softly that if I hadn't been watching I probably wouldn't have noticed.

"My lady." His elbow points towards me and I hook my hand into the crease of his elbow.

"My lord." I give a fake curtsey and we laugh at each other with scrunched noses. I am in the middle of living out some rom-com and it makes my heart burst.

Once we reach the bottom floor, the elevator doors open and my face flushes. I have never been good with crowds, let alone a crowd full of people that I have to fake enjoy for the next two hours. My mind goes blank when I see the different faces of people I recognize, all congregating in the main area of the hotel, waiting for the doors to open to the reception hall.

All I hear is a ringing and fuzzy voice, none of which I can discern from each other. With each moment, the voices become more and more distant. I no longer feel Jordan holding me upright; my whole entire body feels like it's buzzing. The only thing I can clearly hear is my heartbeat, which feels like it is in my chest. I know this feeling all too well, this panicking, it happens every so often and I have no control of it coming or passing.

The last time this happened was only two days ago at my

birthday party. My parents asked me repeatedly if I had gotten a full-time job, as if full-time school and a part-time job wasn't good enough. The disappointment in their voices reminded me of the disappointment I felt all throughout growing up. I was never allowed to complain about my home situation to friends, because my parents were comfortable financially, but that didn't mean that the constant pressure for my grades to always be better, the job I had in high school to pay more, the way I was not succeeding enough ever, it didn't mean that those situations didn't stick with me.

I had to relearn to be proud of myself without the need for their approval. Moving out was an eternal struggle, because nowhere that I could afford would ever get their stamp of approval and I knew that.

Jordan was still holding onto me, and I had to free myself to run to the nearest restroom, luckily avoiding the crowd. I abandoned Jordan right outside of the elevator doors, and every move, every single thing I did between then and splashing my face with water was a blur.

The restroom door opens as I dry my face with the brown paper towels from the wall, trying to dab lightly to not ruin my makeup.

"Anna? Is that you?" Jamie Longwood grabs my hand, only heightening my anxiety.

"Jamie!" I put my pretend excited face on. Jamie and I stayed by each other's side all throughout eighth grade, and while I'm upset that anyone walked in on me looking like such a mess, it could have been worse.

"Are you ok? Do you need help?" Without my response, Jamie grabs the paper towel from me and fixes the mascara that sat on my face from the splashing I did at the sink.

"Thank you. I'm sorry, I just had a little panicky feeling in the crowd. I'll be ok though." My smile is slightly crooked, but hopefully convincing. "I'll go grab a piece of toilet paper from a stall and clean myself up, thank you for your help." I was very grateful; she is still one of the sweetest people I know, all these years later.

The door bursts open with extreme force again and this time I hear a familiar voice as I stand in the stall grabbing the tissue from the giant roll.

"Where is she?" The growl is something I have never heard before, the breathing in between each word stronger every time.

"This is the girls' room, get out, sicko!" Jamie squeals and I immediately step out of the stall. Knowing Jamie, she would have pepper spray or something on her that Jordan would not walk out unscathed from.

"I'm ok, I'm ok." I hold my hands up in surrender, hoping it calms the storm I can almost physically see rising in his chest.

"Annie. Oh my gosh, you scared me."

I'm immediately enveloped in a warm hug, my head lying flat on his chest, my arms squeezing tight against his waist. His lips meet my forehead, before we realize we aren't alone.

"Woah, I did not see that coming." Jamie's voice is shocked, rightfully so. I didn't see myself finding comfort in Jordan Myers either.

Releasing myself from his hold, I let out a little laugh at Jamie's thoughts. "Me neither, Jamie, me neither." My voice is starting to calm, and I realize that Jordan has now turned in the direction of Jamie with me, putting his hands in his pockets, as he always does.

"Hey!" Jordan gives a sarcastic tone as he speaks. It makes my breathing naturally calm, watching his face light up like that.

"Don't run off on me like that, I got scared." The growl leaves and changes to a voice of worry.

"I'll see you guys out there." I'm glad Jamie realizes that this is a moment we need by ourselves, she's already halfway out the door before letting us know.

"I'm sorry, I know I just… I… I guess I don't know what happened. I get panicky sometimes and sometimes it makes me feel like I'm going to die, and I just needed to get out of there."

His thumb wipes the tears falling on my face, the overwhelming feeling finally leaving my body in the form of tears.

"You were having a panic attack. I just don't want you to think I can't help you through them. What are friends for if not to help each other calm each other down?"

I laugh as I press my head further into his palm. "Panic attacks are for people with anxiety, and I sir, do not have anxiety." I get anxious, sure, but having a whole diagnosis for a few freak outs a month is not something I need right now.

"Annie, have you ever talked to someone about them? The panicky feelings?"

I shake my head at his question. I have thought about bringing it up at many previous appointments with my physician, but I've never actually gone through with it.

"You should make an appointment, and tell someone, if not for yourself, for me."

My head shakes in the opposite direction now. He's right, I should, I just never thought it was worth it before.

After some deep breathing together, he guides me with his hand out of the bathroom. Most of the crowd is gone; the hall doors have been opened.

"If it gets too much, just tell me, we'll have a code word or something. Grapefruit."

"Grapefruit?" I hold a smile from climbing on my face. "You want me to randomly tell you Grapefruit, and then you'll save me." The smile didn't cooperate very well, as now it's grinning ear to ear. "No way, let's use…" I rack my brain for any other word but Grapefruit. "Butterflies," I say, keeping our elongated eye contact.

"Butterflies." He has no clue what the word means to me, but hearing him say it makes them appear again.

We make our way to the hall, it's decorated gorgeously: navy and gold waves of fabric from the ceiling, round tables covered with white satin table coverings.

"Wow."

All I receive from Jordan is a smile, and yet again he guides me with his hand at the small of my back. We weave through the tables, people sitting at every chair. Jamie is sitting with three people at a table in the back. I don't recognize any of them, but since I know Jamie, I think I would feel most comfortable there.

My finger points in the direction of the table, and luckily Jordan understands and we continue to bob through the crowd effortlessly. He seems to always know what I need, more importantly what I want, unless you count him punching Jace in the face. I did not in fact want that.

Once we get to the table, Jordan pulls out the chair nearest to Jamie for me. We hug as he pushes my seat in.

"Sorry we didn't say much earlier, I was kind of having a moment." I laugh as I pull my arms back from her black sequined dress.

"I could tell, so you have to spill! What's the deal with you two?" She whispers the last half of her sentence as if Jordan wasn't going to be able to hear from one chair away.

"He's my um…well…"

Jordan interrupts swiftly. "Boyfriend, I'm her boyfriend." He squeezes my leg, just above my knee, an indication that I need to keep myself together.

"Wait, seriously? Last I heard, you guys were trying to kill each other. What happened?" Jamie is just as confused as I am, I don't think I could've ever imagined sitting here wishing Myers would never take his hand off of me.

"Actually, I got locked out of my apartment, and he offered to let me stay at the hotel he owns. Castino's." We may have met at the grocery store, but I don't think that is quite as romantic as offering to save a woman from sleeping on the streets.

"It was the least I could do. I ruined her favorite T-shirt at the grocery store before that, I kind of owed her one." Jordan places a kiss onto my cheek, as if he had been telling people this story for years. This feels so natural, Jordan sitting next to me, telling people how we rekindled, the cheek, everything, and my heart ached for when we got home. It would all be over.

A familiar face comes back from the punch bowl: Lyla McCloud.

"Oh my gosh! Is that Annabelle?!" She rushes over to my seat and hugs me from behind. Lyla and I were never as close as Jamie and I were. She was one of those overly optimistic people, so we could never tell her our problems without her trying to find a silver lining.

"Lyla! Good to see you." I squeeze her arm that's wrapped around my neck, using my left hand. My other hand is squeezing Jordan's wrist tight enough that I probably left a bruise.

"Lyla, I haven't seen you in years. How are you?" Jordan chimes in, which urges Lyla to switch from me to him, hugging him in a similar fashion. His face jerks and I can see he's uncomfortable, I've never seen him look quite like that, and it makes me choke on a sip of water I had taken.

"Jordan Myers, wow, what a guy. I never thought you would've come to this type of thing." Her voice squeaks in my ears, reminding me why I didn't hang out with her quite as often as Jamie.

"I usually wouldn't, but I was dragged by my lady."

I roll my eyes at this statement. Me dragging him? Very funny. I wasn't the one who showed up at his doorstep with a matching T-shirt.

"Oh my gosh, I can't wait to meet her. Did she come today?"

Letting out the biggest laugh ever, Jordan plants a fat one on me. My anxiety shoots through the roof. I just found out that PDA is not my thing.

Everyone's eyes widen, and I make an uncomfortable face as I pull from the kiss. I try not to offend Jordan with my expression, but I could tell he wasn't happy with what I had just done.

"I think you already know her." His voice has the slightest hint of disdain in it. I can tell what I did after we kissed upset him.

Lyla's face shoots to mine and she mouths the words "Shut up," to me. I've learned that a lot of people can't really believe who I ended up with.

Idaho is known for people marrying young. Lyla sat next to her husband Jon; Jamie next to her husband Adam. If you weren't engaged, or in a serious relationship at this point in my life, people thought you were going to be alone forever.

"So, how long have you been together?" Questions about our relationship start pouring in, and I realize we should have prepared a little better.

"2 years."

"2 months." Jordan and I say at the exact same time.

I correct myself to match him. "2 years." Hopefully that got them off my backs.

"2 years, and no proposal. What's the hold up, Jordan?"

I dart my eyes toward him in a panicked fashion.

"Oh, we just don't have the rings yet, we actually got engaged last week."

The panic starts to show on my face. Engaged? We had talked about a fake relationship, but now we have to fake an engagement? This is too much for me.

"Wait… I thought you said you were her boyfriend earlier." Jamie chimes back into the conversation.

"Sorry, it's still so fresh, I forget I get to keep this one forever now." He really says this stuff so easily it's amazing.

"Yep." I curl my lips in on themselves. "Can't help it, the man just gives me butterflies." I look over to Jordan to make sure he gets the message.

Once the questioning dies a little bit, Jordan takes my hand and excuses us both from the table. "We're going to get a drink, does anyone want anything?"

Everyone shakes their head no, and relief hits. We make our way to the refreshment table where another white tablecloth sits.

"Engaged? Are you nuts?" I hit him with my clutch on the side of his arm.

"I'm sorry, I panicked when everyone was talking about marriage and how weird it was that we were in such a 'long' relationship without a proposal, it seemed natural." He raises his arms trying to convince me this was not his fault.

"What am I supposed to do now, we don't know each other well enough to pull this off."

His eyes watch the words come out of my mouth. "Is that

what this is about? You don't think we know each other well enough? Is that why you were so upset when I kissed you back there?" Our voices are now yelling in a whisper, and people don't seem to notice.

"That is not why I didn't like you kissing me. I very much liked you kissing me, I just didn't realize I don't like PDA, especially when it comes to kissing." I'm shaking fingers in his face and anger begins to climb throughout my body. Did he really not think I liked kissing him? Of course I did, I just didn't like that I could feel other eyes on us.

"Right, it was the PDA, of course." He shakes his head and makes his way towards the exit.

"Wait, come on, that is not fair, you know how I am with people." I follow him, trying not to shout as we leave.

"I know how you are with people Annie, I just thought I was different. The fact is, I know how you are with people because I know you; I know you don't like crowds, or shirts that are too short, I know you like when I put my hand on your lower back, and I know you are weirdly obsessed with Donny Osmond. I know you are self-conscious about how your hair lays, so you mainly wear it up, unless it's a special occasion. You throw out all the orange Gushers because you think they taste different, even though they really don't. And I thought I knew how you felt about me, but I guess I was wrong about that one."

I stop dead in my tracks.

"What do you mean, how I feel about you?" My voice softens and is no longer yelling.

Frustrated, Jordan turns back towards me. "I thought…I thought that after that morning we had breakfast there was something, I don't know, a spark or…or whatever you want to call it."

All I want to shout is butterflies, they are butterflies. He looked so defeated, now was not the time to try and correct him.

"Jordan I…" Why couldn't I just tell him how I feel! Why would I not do that? I ask myself over and over again until I realize he's already heading back towards the elevators.

I try to call out for him, but it's no use. This was entirely my fault. I could have just gone along with the whole engagement thing, and now I have to suffer the consequences of possibly losing Jordan forever.

Putting my best smile on I head back to the reception area and sit next to Jamie.

"Sorry, Jordan wasn't feeling well, he went back to his room." I wanted to say anything before the questions came in.

"Anna, are you ok? You seem a little flushed."

She's probably right, I don't feel very well. This is something I had never felt before. Sad butterflies.

Chapter 9

Alone

I had gotten used to having someone around me at all times. Jamie told me to head back to my room and gave me her new phone number so that we could connect. It turns out she lives right by the Walmart I go to. My dress dragged against the floor as I made my way to the elevator, its red fabric scraping the ground since I took my heels off.

I carried the shoes by the three-inch sticks and swung them as I walked through the lobby.

"Miss, are you ok?" The attendant at the front desk getting my attention.

Lies arise from my mouth. I seem to always either be lying to people, or not speaking at all, and it's beginning to cause some problems. "I'm fine, I think it's just some food poisoning." Food poisoning? Really? Now this man thinks I'm either throwing up or having explosive diarrhea. Very attractive.

His face shows his worry, but I don't continue the conversation. I'm not exactly looking to talk about the different side effects of having food poisoning right now.

Once I reach the elevator, I hit the arrow and wait for it to arrive patiently. My room is on the third floor, room 308. The same room number I had the night Jordan let me stay in his hotel.

The elevator doors open, and Jordan is standing inside. He has changed back into the clothes he wore on the way here, and he doesn't even look up. He's acting like the past month hasn't happened at all.

I close my eyes and sigh as he pushes past me. Our shoulders barely touch and it feels so much more cold and distant than it has throughout our recent history. I can't believe what is happening right now. It feels like everything that has happened just imploded right in front of me, and I have no one to blame but myself.

I am in fact alone again.

Chapter 10

Revisiting

The next morning, I wake up and pack my things that are scattered in my room. I have no idea how I'm going to get home; there is no way that Jordan is going to take me. Once my things are in my suitcase, I stuff them down and draw the zipper. I look at the Donny Osmond shirt that Jordan had given me. Pulling it over my head, I stare at myself in my bathroom mirror, I look so dissolved.

Mascara stained my already heavy eye bags and made them appear deeper. My energy was so depleted last night all I did was change into a tank top and shorts and fall asleep. I used my last makeup remover to wipe over my face trying to take off any trace of pigment left on my skin.

Using the bar of soap that is provided by the hotel, I wash my face to take anything left off of my face before drying it with a towel. The fibers run across my skin, making my already sensitive skin burn. I'm not a high-quality gal, but the least they could have done is put in hand towels that wouldn't make my face feel like I had taken a sanding block to it.

I have special lotion for when my face gets irritated like this. I got it from a dermatologist when I was on Accutane for some intense pubescent years. I usually only have to use it in the winter, but I guess this is a good excuse.

I take about a pump and a half and smear it more intensely

than I should. I should really try and be more careful with my skin. It's never going to be flawless if I treat it like crap.

The clerk downstairs shows me to a car outside that has been ordered for me.

"Thank you, here are the key cards." This is a different clerk than last night. I'm assuming both work part time.

"I'm sorry, but I didn't pay for this…I think there may be a mistake."

The clerk turns to face me again. "Oh, I'm sorry, are you not Annabelle Richards?" His voice sounds confused.

"I am, I just didn't pay for it, and to be honest, I can't afford it."

The only response I get is, "It's been paid for."

Everything in my mind clicks. Jordan would rather pay hundreds of dollars for me to ride five hours in a car with a complete stranger than be near me. Mr. Laylock, the chauffeur, grabs my things and I spend the next few hours in silence as we make our way back to Wallace. I held in the tears that were begging to be let go.

"What apartment is yours? I'll bring your bags up for you, miss." He is looking through the rearview mirror, waking me from my two-hour nap.

"No need, I'll bring them up myself."

"Are you sure? It's no trouble at all."

I start yawning deeply before I can respond. "Yeah, I'm actually going straight to another apartment so it's no big deal."

I can see the reflection of his nod as he pulls into a spot right near the lobby entrance.

"Thank you for the ride, I'm sorry it was so last minute." I did truly feel sorry. Typically for this type of ride, you need a week's notice, maybe more.

He nods and tips his hat towards me as I gather my bag from the trunk. Laylock hands me a card with his information, along with small print that asks to rate him five stars.

"Will do." I raise the card to let him know the reference.

He thanks me and I head toward the doors.

I stop by my apartment first to set my bag inside. I toss it gently on the floor near my couch and immediately leave. A scent hits me as I walk back through the door frame, it smells like eucalyptus and mint. Some Old Spice deodorant lingers as well.

The feeling comes back, not the butterflies, the panic. What have I done? I let my anxiety and fears get the best of me, and it's going to cost me deeply.

Through the blur that is my mind, I somehow manage to finish locking my apartment door and make my way down the hall towards the elevator. The doors open briefly with a deep chime to indicate it has arrived on my floor.

Georgia Hidi is inside. She looks so much better than previously; light is in her eyes, and she seems like she could conquer the world. Her face makes every ounce of panic fade. It had been so long since I had seen her up and around, it makes my heart ring with joy.

"Georgia! Oh my gosh, you look amazing!"

Her face smiles at the sound of my voice. "You know, I'm not supposed to be talking to you." Her voice is shaky, and slightly sarcastic. These feel like old friends, and I forget that they are also Jordan's grandparents.

"Right…" I don't think if I were them, I would want to talk to me either.

"Can I give you some advice?" Georgia pushes the button to floor four.

I shake my head hesitantly. The advice I need right now is

not something I think she can give me.

"I've been around for a long time, like, a long time." She giggles at her words. "When a boy, excuse me, a man lays all of his feelings out there for you, maybe don't just sit there in silence." Jordan must have told her what I had done, and yet again, I can't blame him.

"You know, I didn't mean to hurt him. I was just so shocked, I thought he was doing this all for show, for the reunion…When he said that he thought there was something there, my mind just slipped into a blur."

Georgia reaches for my hand and gives it a soft southern squeeze. I watch her carefully exit as the door chimes once more.

Never in my life did I think I would have gotten advice from Georgia Hidi about Jordan Myers.

I slowly exit behind her and stop one door away from hers and knock. It's Sunday. Russ and Laura should be home. I knock hard enough that my knuckles are red; I don't think I've ever wanted to be in their apartment more than right now.

Russ frantically opens the door and watches me collapse with emotion the minute I see his face. I ran into his chest for the biggest hug I have ever received. His blonde curls entangle with my black artificial ones as he places a kiss on the top of my head.

"Russ…I…" I'm gasping for air in between words as my shoulders shake. "I screwed up."

He raises my head to meet his eyes, and I see Laura standing behind him with her arms folded, and pity across her face.

"You were the douche canoe." Russ lightly laughs as he whispers to me.

"I was the douche canoe." My words lighten ever so softly, but the tears are still coming down my face at an accelerated pace.

Laura finally switches places with Russ and embraces me as

she simultaneously guides me to the couch. I plop on their dark green cushion and allow Laura to gently stroke my back as I recount what I had done.

"I just stood there, like an idiot while the guy basically professed his love for me."

Russ nods as I tell my story. He makes his way into the kitchen and pulls a Diet Coke from the fridge.

"I'm ok, thank you." I wave my hand slightly to refuse the gesture. I don't think in my twenty-three years of life I have ever refused a Diet Coke, but the thought of it makes me sick. All I see when the bottle appears is Jordan about to take a sip and then kissing me.

"Wow, Jordan really messed you up."

I put my elbows to my knees to let Laura know what she is doing is soothing. "It's not even his fault. I shouldn't have second guessed him." My crying has stopped, but my voice has become hoarse due to the crying.

"Anna, why don't you just tell him? You know where he lives, you should go to Castino's and get him back."

I had already thought about this scenario, but I don't know what I would do if I got there and he dismissed me.

"I can't. What if he decides I'm not worth it, what if he decides that I screwed up too badly? I can't... I just can't."

Russ looks at me with a confused face. "So what? So what if he decides that, then it's on him not you. You deserve to have some kind of closure either way, right?"

I guess Russ is probably right. I may be a douche canoe, but I am a douche canoe that deserves some type of closure.

"Tomorrow, I'll go tomorrow. I need a day to think about what I'm going to say." The plan is now in place. I just have to think about how I'm going to execute it.

"That's the plan, then: you'll stay here tonight, and we'll all come up with a plan on how to get your man back."

I laugh. My man. Jordan is anything but my man right now. That is exactly what I plan to change.

My shoes click as I pace back and forth in Russ and Laura's kitchen, creating an echo against the appliances. "Should I just tell him? Like say 'Jordan I'm an idiot, please take me back?'" My fingers rub against my chin as I nod at the thought.

"Anna, please don't do that, you'll make him run for the hills."

Laura hits Russ's chest with the back of her hand, creating a thud in the living room.

"Annabelle." I cringe at my name. "All you need to do is tell him you're sorry, and that you know that he didn't deserve the way he was treated, but that you were scared. Tell him the truth."

Truth is good, I can do truth.

I rub both of my hands on my face, pulling and stretching at my eyes and mouth. "I don't think I can do this. I'm terrified." Russ shoots me a look, almost like I couldn't have said anything worse. "Can I talk to you for a second? Alone?"

Why does Russ need to talk to me alone? Laura knows the whole situation, she probably knows better than I do at this point. I know they have all talked to Jordan since ironing things out.

My head slowly nods and I make my way into Laura's office.

"Listen, I love you, Anna, you know I do, but even if you don't end up with Jordan, I really need you to get on good terms with him, OK?"

I'm sure he can see the surprise on my face. "Why do you care? You guys just became friends like two seconds ago?"

Russ raises a finger to his lips to get me to talk softer. "I told him about something, and he is the only reason I'll be able to afford what I talked to him about. It was almost a peace offering."

Did they join the mafia together? Why are they making secret deals that Laura and I can't know?

"What are you talking about….Woah!"
Russel pulls a black velvet box from his jean pocket, hushing me as he opens it. "This was my mom's ring. My dad gave it to me when she passed away, and I've held onto it ever since. With our anniversary coming up, I wanted to surprise her."

Russ's mom passed away the year after we graduated high school. He rarely talked about her; I'm sure it still feels like she got in the car crash yesterday. The diamond was oval cut, a gold band, simple but elegant.

"She is going to love this." My eyes are gawking at the ring; it's gorgeous, she really is so lucky. "And about time!" I playfully hit the side of his arm. They've been together for almost four years, and I know she's been dying for a ring.

"I know you don't really like jewels, but I wanted to know your thoughts." Russ is probably going to be the only reason I actually get a ring I like. My family has many generations of Scottish family history, and all I've ever wanted is a Celtic knot ring. It represents unity and eternity. The whole reason it's a knot is that it never ends.

"Russ, I don't think you could have done any better. She loves the simple stuff, you know that."

He nods his head and tries to close the box as softly as possible.

"Wait… so what does Jordan have to do with this?" There's no way he is a groomsman or something like that, he and I will have to fight to the death for that spot as best man.

"He… he told me we could use the hotel for the wedding for free. The prices of venues are skyrocketing and we could really use the help."

Russ didn't need to say anymore. There was no way I was going to let my boy problems stand in the way of Russ and Laura's eternal happiness.

"I'll talk to him tomorrow. I promise. I'm so proud of you."

We hug once more before exiting the room. I have to control the emotions on my face when I see Laura come back with plates of food she must have whipped up. Russ gives me side eye galore before I'm finally able to contain my excitement.

"I think I'm OK to go home. I should probably think by myself for a minute anyway. I'll let you know what happens tomorrow."

They need some time alone before their pending engagement. Hearing that news made every ounce of stress and negativity wash away.

"Are you sure? You can stay if you'd like," Laura chimes in after grabbing my stained plate from the ravioli she handed me.

"I'm really ok, and guys…I missed you. I'm sorry."

Both of their faces meet mine before saying in precise unison, "We missed you too."

It felt incredible to be missed.

I make my way to the door and turn the knob slowly. I turn one last time to Russ and give him a wink that makes his cheeks glow. I've never met two people who are meant for each other more than these two.

At my apartment I rehearse over and over what I'm going to say. "Jordan, I know you're mad but…no that's not it." I run my fingers through my hair in pure frustration. "Jordan, I'm sorry, when you talked about the spark I panicked. My anxiety was already high and…I feel the same way." Sure, that would have to do. Hopefully it will get him to do something.

Chapter 11

Forgiveness

My alarm wakes me up at seven A.M. This time I let it play on a loop as I rush around my apartment getting ready. For a second, I thought maybe I should put on my green dress and makeup. If I can't get him with my words, might as well make him speechless with the rest of me.

I look in the mirror at the clothes I already have on. My own Hard Rock Boise shirt and a pair of jeans. This was it. This was me in a nutshell. Would I really want someone who would only take me if I dressed up? I may look ridiculously good in green, and maybe even better in red according to Jordan, but it wasn't who I was. I was the girl that hid in her apartment and sang to the Spongebob Squarepants musical episodes and ate Gushers like they were a life source. I was not the girl that tried to win over a man with a gown.

Waking up this early made my eye bags look like they were from a wholesale store on sale. Despite my best effort, I touch a few dabs of concealer under my eyes and swipe them using my cold fingers.

"Ok douche canoe, it's now or never."

I down a pack of Gushers in my mouth before I head towards my door. Somehow, they give me more confidence. I don't understand it, but I don't think I really need to.

The stairs creak as I take one step after another. Stairs were usually the worst part of my apartment, but since knowing Jordan, I find myself doing all sorts of strange things, like taking the stairs, turning down soda, and even drinking *gag* water.

This man was making me turn into a healthy human being.

"He may take away my soda, but he will never take away my Gushers." My voice is quiet and shaky as I hurdle myself down the disgusting and stained steps. I find myself smiling over an imaginary argument over my overall sugar intake. I would love to argue with him, I would love to even just talk with him again.

I have never been in a serious relationship before. I've gone on dates, even dated someone for about six months, but it didn't feel like this. This felt like something that was always meant to happen. Like every single time we fought or made comments in the past ten years was leading to this.

The wind that touches my skin as soon as I hit the outdoors gives me a chill. It usually doesn't get this cold this early in the year, and I wasn't really prepared for it. My goosebumps that crawled on my skin became sharp as I tried to warm myself. If they really wanted to, it felt like they could cut me.

My Elantra sat in my assigned spot, a little dust sat on the hood. I hadn't realized how long it had been since I had driven it. I pull the bottom of my shirt up and wipe a slab of dust to the ground, exposing the dull paint beneath it, barely reflecting in the sun.

The dust that kicks in my face makes me cough as I walk around to the driver's side.

"It might be time to turn in, Baxter, you're getting old."

Baxter was already used when my parents gifted him to me when I was sixteen. After almost ten years of using him, he had gotten to the point of no return.

My door handle catches as I try to open the door to the steering wheel. I pull with enough strength that my tendons stick out from the inside of my wrist. Finally, the door gives way, and the fight leaves me out of breath.

"Now is not the time to act up, Baxter, we've got work to do." I play the usual game of shutting my door repeatedly before it sticks. Once it does, I put my car in reverse and leave the complex.

The heartbeat running through my ears reminds me of what I am about to do. I had been disturbingly positive the majority of the morning, as if this was just a casual run for errands.

Usually on car rides I have my radio blasting, A/C pushing my hair around the cabin, and a big smile on my face. Car rides were a way for me to calm my entire system without having to think too much about what I was doing.

This time I had the A/C off, my radio silenced and the look of concentration in my eyes. This was a serious matter.

My breathing quickens once I'm within a block of the hotel. The only way I seem to calm myself down is imagining Jordan talking to me. He is the only one in the past twenty-three years of my life that has ever been able to calm the neurotic side of me.

My car pulls to a stop in the front of guest parking, right in front of the automatic doors. Inhale, exhale. My mind can be crazy, but I can't let the crazy show.

In any other town you wouldn't leave anything important in the car, but the worst someone could steal from me in this car is the keys, which at this point makes no difference to me. I throw myself into park and check my pulse. I guess it's running around one-hundred-ten, but I haven't had to check pulses in a long time.

The confidence I once had has weakened the more I have sat here, but I can't stay here much longer or I may not go in.

The Elantra's door creaks open and I slam it closed with just the right amount of force for it to close on the first try.

A whirring occurs as the doors slide themselves open and I immediately take note of Kira's eyes on me.

"Kira! Oh, thank goodness, I need to see Jordan, where is he?"

Her mouth opens, but no words come out.

"Kira…please." My guess is she's been told to not let me in explicitly.

"He um…he isn't taking visitors right now. You'll have to come back."

A grunt escapes me. Not taking visitors, or not taking me?

A familiar face takes the corner. Jace is standing there.

"Jace, hi." We haven't seen each other or spoken since he claims I took heartbreak off his list.

"Hi, Anna, um… Kira's right, Jordan isn't taking any visitors right now."

I cross the lobby and hold onto the side of his arm. "Jace, please." I'm pleading with him, and I can feel tears form in my eyes, but I have to force myself to keep them to myself.

"I can't, I would if I could, I hope you know that." Jace turns to Kira as if to ask for any form of support, but I don't think she knows what to do either.

"Fine." My back turns to the both of them admitting defeat, but I turn quickly and duck under Jace's arm.

They both chase me as I break into a jog, yelling at me to stop.

I take a sharp corner and I am met at the door that floods my body with memories. I curl my hand into a fist and knock with extreme purpose. Jace and Kira are too late, and they stop midway down the hall.

The door slowly opens. "Kira, I told you I can't have anyone…"

"Hi." My voice is soft as I look at the scruff he had built on his face over the past forty-eight hours. "I just wanted to…"

"Anna, now is not a good time." His voice is deep and frustrated. The tone is deserved, but what really sticks out is the name he calls me. I would get on my hands and knees for him to call me Annie.

"Please, just one minute." My facial expressions soften as I observe his motions.

I do not get a reply. Instead, a shock sends through my body as he shuts the door in my face.

The vibrations cause my body to react in the one way I had been hoping to avoid. Tears start streaming and it seems like I have lost the fight to hold myself together. My nose is running and eyes wet. I take the back of my hand and wipe both areas.

Jace peeks around the corner, still handsome, but this time he looks sad. "Anna, I told you…he—"

The door opens once more, and my eyes lift. "You must be Annie."

Chapter 12

The Myers

Before me is a tall slender woman in an ivory button down and slick black satin pencil skirt. She looks in her 60s, but I couldn't tell anyone for sure.

"I am." I reach out my hand to shake hers, but it's rejected. "Actually, it's Annabelle."

She scans my body before speaking again. "Annabelle, cute, very quaint. Come in." She opens the door wide enough that I can see Jordan in his signature office chair sitting at his desk, eyes glued to the floor. I don't know who this woman is, but she obviously thinks she has the authority to invite me into Jordan's office.

"Jordan, can I?" It only feels like the right thing to do to ask the actual owner for permission.

He looks up from the ground and waves to fingers for me to enter.

Shutting the door behind me, I notice someone who was once hidden by the oak of the door. A man about the same age stands in a custom suit and holds out a hand to me.

"Larry, Larry Myers. And my wife, Carmen. We've heard a lot about you, Annabelle."

My eyes grow in size. Holy crap. These are Jordan's parents.

I shoot a look at Jordan, who is just as stunned as I am.

"Wow, I um…I've heard lots about you as well." They didn't

need to know most of what I heard wasn't good.

Larry sits back down in his chair and Carmen follows next to him. They both groan at my comment. Maybe they don't need to know what I've heard isn't good, they know based on what they've done.

"I can come back. I was just trying to talk to Jordan is all." I really wanted to talk to him, but I didn't want to use the word douche canoe in front of his parents.

"No, no, don't be silly, we'll leave you alone. We just wanted to make plans with our son." Jordan watches his father spit out the word son as if he had taken a dagger to him. My heart twists in tune with his.

"Son? I'm sorry, I don't know either of you well, but I do know enough to know you do not under any circumstances get to call this man son. You do not get to prey on his success just because it is convenient to you. He has everything he has ever needed and more, *despite* the way he was treated by either of you."

Jordan looks at me, mouth wide open. My heart is beating faster than ever before. I have never once in my life raised my voice at someone I just met, but this was the exception.

My hand automatically reaches for the doorknob to his office.

"Annie, stay. They need to leave." This is the first time he has spoken since I've entered the room. His figure grows as he stands towering over the desk in front of him. "Larry, Carmen, it was nice to meet you, but I think it's time for you to go back to Florida." His voice growls as if a command more than a suggestion.

I watch both of his parents rise and gather their things.

"Jordan, please." Carmen pleads with her child.

Jordan doesn't give them the dignity of a verbal response, but instead shakes his head.

I step out of the way and let them pass through the door. My eyes meet Jordan's again. "I'll go too."

I turn back towards the door to exit when a hand grabs my wrist behind me. My body almost naturally turns at this point, almost like I have been doing ballet my entire life.

"Stay." The growl of command has grown.

My eyes are wet again, I don't know what I'm about to say, but I know that my eyes won't be dry as I speak.

"Jordan. I am so sorry. When you said there was a spark, I didn't know how to react. I got so scared that I panicked and my whole body shut down, but I want to be with you. I want to be with you so much I didn't have a Diet Coke at Russ's last night, and I took the stairs this morning. I want...I need you."

His face is focused on every word I say and I can't tell whether or not he has decided it's too late. "Annie, I didn't leave because I was mad. Well...I was mad, but that's not why I left. My parents showed up unannounced a few days ago asking Kira for my information. It didn't feel right leaving her to deal with them. But when I got here, all they wanted was a share in the hotel. They didn't want me, or even my money. They wanted to buy me out. I hadn't spoken to them my entire life, and they had the audacity to ask for my business." He drops my hand and I watch as his own tears fill his eyes, changing the color from white to red.

I don't say a single thing, but instead grab his face with both of my hands. My thumb wipes his tears every time one falls, and I finally kiss his cheek, too cold for comfort.

"They don't deserve to know you, Jordan Myers. They don't deserve any piece of you."

Chapter 13

Butterflies

Jordan and I sit across from each other at the diner, watching each other carefully.

"You know, I did think there was a spark or whatever at the breakfast that first night." He plays with his food as he embarrassingly speaks.

I drop my grilled cheese on the plate in front of me and the waiter refills my second Diet Coke. "Butterflies, there were butterflies." I corrected his term.

He puts down his knife and fork and grabs both sides of my face across the table. "Annabelle Richards, you give me butterflies."

My smile grows wide as he kisses me and I catch the taste of his diner steak in my mouth.

"Butterflies?" My voice influxes at the question

"Butterflies." Jordan sits back in the booth and we watch each other eat.